DISMAL DREAMS

Red Lagoe

DISMAL DREAMS

Edited by Gabino Iglesias

Cover and interior art ©2021 Red Lagoe

ISBN (paperback): 978-0-9988531-5-4
ISBN (e-book): 978-0-9988531-6-1

la
red
LaRed Books

PREVIOUSLY PUBLISHED STORIES:

Creation of Man: originally published at redlagoe.com, 2020

Flicker: originally published in *If I Die Before I Wake: Tales of Karma and Fear* by Sinister Smile Press, 2019

A Cold Day in Hell: originally published in *Shiver, A Chilling Horror Anthology,* edited by Nico Bell, 2021

Valentine's Day: originally published at redlagoe.com, 2020

Prospect Nowhere: originally published in *Dark Moon Digest, issue 38*, by Perpetual Motion Machine Publishing, 2020

One Year Anniversary: originally published in *Slashertorte: An Anthology of Cake Horror* by Sliced Up Press, 2020

Never Have I Ever: originally published in *If I Die Before I Wake: Tales of Supernatural Horror* by Sinister Smile Press, 2020

Doll House: originally published in *We Are Wolves* by Burial Day Books, 2020

For my pandemic homies:

Jason, Niam, & Jack

TABLE OF CONTENTS

FOREWORD
by Sara Tantlinger

"Allison didn't have to cut herself open to know she was pretty on the inside."

Do I have your attention? That line certainly grabbed mine, but then again, Red Lagoe so keenly held my fascination throughout the entire collection of *Dismal Dreams*. Sharp lines, clever plots, and strong characters are only a few of the exciting elements you will find infused into each story. The quote above is from "Doll House"—originally published by Burial Day Books in *We Are Wolves*—and it's wonderful to see the story again here because it fits *Dismal Dreams* so well. Within, Lagoe takes us on many journeys, and like in "Doll House", we discover themes of womanhood rooted deeply in horror, of how the decisions we need to make to survive may end up being costly, and bloody, in the end.

One of my favorites in the collection—"Creation of Man"— offers a fascinating take on Adam and Eve. It's a clever, dark little thing, and Lagoe is just so good at spinning expectations of a story's premise or trope and taking it into a direction that is entirely her own. "Vengeance is born of the earth," Lagoe writes in this tale of snakes and bones and jealousy. Later in the collection, vengeance does strike again, and the way Lagoe executes these plot points remains satisfying even long after closing the book.

Dismal Dreams is a strong follow-up to *Lucid Screams.* From reading both collections, it's apparent how much fun Lagoe has with her storytelling, and how much thought she puts into her craft.

The first story of *Dismal Dreams* is the title story, and immediately we are shown something grim, gritty, and full of heart. That focus on what dwells within the deepest fear of one's heart becomes a central theme overall in the collection. The characters we meet are often full of dreams and wants, and sometimes they have to take unusual routes to find success (as you'll see in "Valentine's Day" and "The Terminator Line" for example). The stakes are high in each story, and it's that focus on conflict that will keep the reader invested from beginning to end.

The characters are also incredibly human, meaning Lagoe expertly taps into what makes people so driven to live and to continue living, even if faced with the grimmest of situations. Familial bonds make appearances in a few stories as well, and as readers we become witnesses to the lengths struggling mothers and fathers will go to in order to protect their child. We also observe the unflinching cruelty other parents are capable of inflicting. The characters open up their wounded souls and we see their desperation, their need to have someone to love, or perhaps how far they might be willing to go to consume the love of a lost partner (as seen in another one of my favorites in here, "One Year Anniversary"). We join these characters as they realize they may need to sever themselves apart in order to find love or reach a goal, how they might find themselves along the way and discover ugly truths, cursed family secrets, or other forbidden knowledge.

There is a great balance of fun and seriousness in *Dismal Dreams*, which I think makes reading a collection all the more enjoyable. That range is certainly on display here, and Lagoe is not afraid to show us that she is willing to take the time to shape the different moods, settings, and characters of these stories to highlight that range. It's easy to fall into a comfortable pace and stay settled in the same atmosphere, but Lagoe isn't interested in easy from what I can tell; instead, she takes us deep into haunted forests where photographers should not tempt the fates, into basements where kidnappings have gone terribly wrong, into the desert where strangeness lurks in unimaginable ways, and so much more.

And, perhaps, Lagoe even takes us to where something rarer lingers—hope. I love a good bleak ending, but when done right, showing those flickers of hope through horror creates such a strong, beautiful feeling, and Lagoe has some tales in here which perfectly capture that spirit. Finding hope in the form of barely escaping alive or perhaps escaping, but with scarlet stains running down from your hands, is a powerful element to convey.

"Burden's Beast"—the final story of the collection—offers hope in a bit of a different way. The tale focuses on the horrific guilt that can stem from witnessing something one is powerless to stop, especially when you're a young girl trying to navigate the world. The emphasis on women reclaiming their lives, their power, it's a strong element throughout Lagoe's stories, and I loved the different ways it was presented. Sometimes that power was used for good and for freedom, and other times for darkness. Creating women who feel real, whether they are trying to survive or are the wicked ones, it keeps the reader deeply invested to see just where Lagoe will take these characters. In "Burden's Beast", we're treated to a richly layered and imaginative tale that bases its horror on realities all too familiar to so many of us, yet the main character's epiphany toward the latter half of the story (I won't give away any spoilers here), is one so worthy of ending a collection with. And you will know that epiphany when you read it.

The story is a powerful conclusion to an exciting collection, and I greatly look forward to what Red Lagoe does next because as she's shown us in *Dismal Dreams,* her craft only gains strength with each new project, and we're really very lucky to have her writing voice in the horror world.

-Sara Tantlinger, Bram Stoker Award-winning author of
The Devil's Dreamland

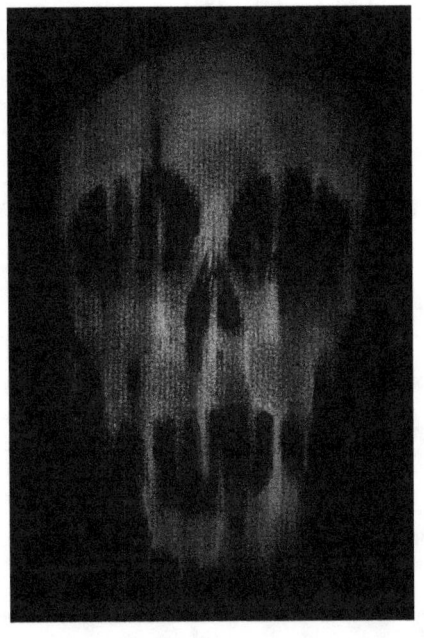

"They've promised that dreams can come true,
but forgot to mention that nightmares are dreams, too."
—*Oscar Wilde*

DISMAL DREAMS

THE GREAT DISMAL SWAMP was said to be haunted. The ghosts of people who had died there supposedly wandered the swamp. Tim wasn't afraid of ghosts though. If anything, they should've been afraid of him. He was a man on a mission. A man ready to reclaim his life.

Tim hadn't taken his kayak out in ages. He didn't do much of anything for himself anymore since Mark was born—hell, not since his wedding—but that was about to change. Back when he was still dating Tanya, he'd been upgrading his kayak little by little. Night lights, rod-holders, GPS navigation system, and a twenty gallon live well. But then life became all work and no play. He'd go to work, come home for dinner, do yard work, fix whatever was broken, then go to bed and repeat. Tanya made plans for every weekend, and like the drone he was, he went wherever she told him to go, did whatever she asked him to do. Then Mark came along and their lives became all about the baby. He loved the little guy, he just needed to get back to his roots. He needed some time to get out on the boat, get back to nature, and be the man he thought he'd grow up to be.

Maple and cypress trees surrounded him as he paddled the feeder ditch that ran three miles through the densely forested swampland. At the end of the man-made canal, sat Lake Drummond, a massive shallow pooling of water smack dab in the middle of the dismal. That's what they called a swamp way back in old times—a dismal.

He'd been to Lake Drummond before, but it'd been years. Dreams of returning someday on a date with his wife became lost in the hectic humdrum of his adult life.

Tim's kayak drifted through marshy waters, out of the feeder ditch and into the open expanse of the lake. Towering cypress trees rose from brackish water and were swallowed by thick fog.

"Why?" Tanya asked from over his shoulder.

Tim closed his eyes and froze. His paddle rested across his lap. Her voice was like a thousand bugs crawling through his head and under his skin. Tim chewed on his lower lip. His racing heart steadied and he wiped the sweat from under his ball cap. The ball cap she'd bought for him.

Tanya was a good wife, and an even better mother. She read up on all the latest baby trends when she was pregnant with Mark. She knew every way to prevent sudden infant death syndrome, and all the best dietary recommendations. She played classical music against her belly. "We have to use black and white," she'd said. "The high contrast is easier for the baby to interpret." Her soft, confident voice stayed in his head as if she were right behind him, whispering into his ear. *"You don't get to raise him."*

"And why not?" he snapped. When he looked over his shoulder, she wasn't there. He found nothing but the thick fog on tea-colored water. Cypress trees loomed over him, their roots raising above the surface like spies, watching his every move, listening to his every word.

"Because you're a murderer," she said.

Tim drifted into the open lake and tucked his paddle to the side.

Trembling hands unlatched the live well, releasing the stench of decaying flesh. He turned his head, holding his breath for a moment so as not to gag.

Inside were tightly packed grocery bags full of Tanya's parts. He hadn't planned on killing her last night. Something snapped. Some long-festering hatred of her incessant planning and packing his life full of things to do—things that were never part of *his* plan. For so long, he'd grin and bear it, not realizing it'd been eating away at him bit by bit. Last night, while Tanya brushed her teeth, giving him yet another task for the next day, something primal rose out of him. An unexpected rage. He grabbed her by the throat. His hands squeezed, locked in place.

That look of fear, shock…the sheer terror in her eyes broke his heart, but not until after she was dead. During…*during*…there was something else in his heart—some survival instinct to take back what was his.

Tanya didn't deserve this, but it was too late for regrets. If he was going to make any of this matter, he had to *live.* Enjoy life for once. It was about time.

So here he was, in the middle of the Dismal Swamp with his wife's body parts in bags. He dropped one bag over the side of the kayak. It sank fast. Though the average depth of Lake Drummond was only about six feet, the bottom was nothing but decaying plant life. Dead leaves, fungus, peat moss. It was soft and swallowed life greedily. Those who fell victim to the mucky trap became food for the cypress trees and bottom feeders.

Tim dropped another bag into the water. He imagined the sawed up body parts sinking into the soil below. His once-precious Tanya becoming new life in the form of a beautiful cypress or lacey Spanish moss. He wondered about all the others who had succumbed to the swamp's death traps. How many became spirits fed into the trees?

One last bag. Through thin plastic, her skull rested in his hands. His stomach lurched.

How did it come to this?

He blamed Tanya. He blamed her for nagging, for keeping his free spirit locked into a domestic life he didn't want, for birthing a child he didn't ask for.

Tim dropped the last of his wife into the swamp and buckled over from the pain in his gut and the pain in his heart.

The paddle back to his vehicle was excruciating. Dark. Silent. Tanya no longer spoke to him from over his shoulder. *No.* He imagined her forever wandering Lake Drummond as some lost, pathetic ghost.

Tim opened the door to his home and was met by the incessant crying of a neglected infant. Mark's screams were desperate. He'd been left alone all day. Tim had no other option. The pulsing dry cry, reminiscent of when Tim let Mark cry it out one day. Tanya had been pissed when she came home to that sound.

Tim pulled a bottle of breast milk from the fridge and warmed it. He opened the nursery door and handed the baby the bottle. Grabbing hands fumbled it into his grip and the baby fed ferociously on his mother's remaining milk. A bulging diaper demanded to be changed, and Tim did his fatherly duties with spite in his heart.

The baby was fed and had a clean diaper, but still cried. He wanted more from Tim. More than Tim could offer. How the hell was he supposed to take care of it? How the hell do people give up everything for someone else? It wasn't fair. It wasn't planned. It shouldn't have to be his responsibility anymore.

Tim looked at the mewling creature who would only take and take and take. Another eighteen years of Tim's life wasted on the happiness of someone other than himself.

He hated it and wanted it to disappear with his wife.

A black veil dropped behind his eyes. A filter allowing him to imagine a life where he could get rid of the baby. He could paddle back to the swamp tonight if he needed to. The hatred and darkness metastasized within and he stumbled out of the nursery to his office.

In the bottom drawer, behind the tax return files, he pulled his lockbox with the handgun. Tanya had insisted he get rid of it with the new baby on the way. Tim told her that he had.

The weight of it in his hand made him feel more powerful than ever. He was the executer of his dreams from this point forward.

The infant screamed across the hall for attention, wanting to be held. Wanting to be the center of Tim's world. But Tim couldn't provide, nor live like this any longer.

Tim lifted the corded receiver from the phone and dialed 9-1-1. His heart galloped wildly, body tremoring. He dropped the receiver and didn't bother picking it back up. Instead, Tim entered the nursery.

From across the hall, the faint sound of a dispatcher's voice answered the call.

Gun in hand, Tim approached the crib. The baby squealed, begging for help.

"You don't deserve him," Tanya whispered.

Tim whipped around, only to see the black and white painted shapes on the walls, memories that Mark once had a mother who did everything she could for him. And what memories would Tim leave for the kid?

He looked into the baby's tear-soaked eyes, its face red with anguish. Tim's lip curled with disgust that he'd never be the man he wanted to be, and he hoped this needy baby would do better with his life than Tim had. Before he could change his mind, Tim pressed the muzzle against his own temple and pulled the trigger.

Blood sprayed from the side of his head and Tim dropped to the floor. The baby silenced only for a moment after the ear-piercing crack of the gunshot. The dispatcher's voice cut out.

The infant stared upon the black and white shapes on the wall. Triangles, circles, squares, all easily interpreted in a baby's developing brain. They were memories of his mother's love. Now, a deep crimson splattered over the shapes, along with the clinging, fleshy bits of his father's brain matter; memories which would settle into the child's subconscious mind and feed his most dismal dreams.

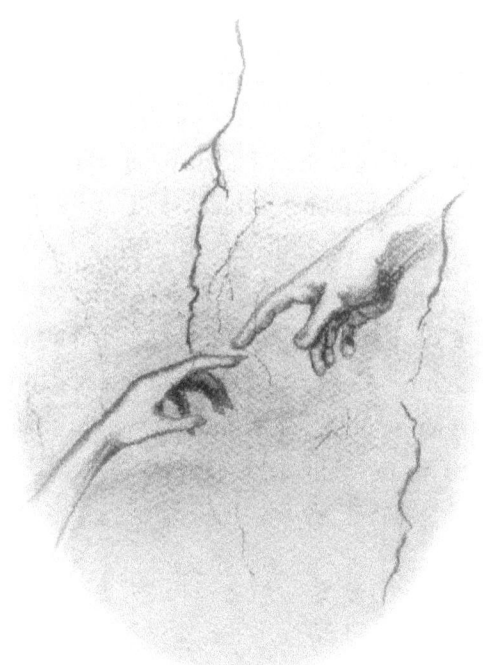

THE CREATION OF MAN

Adam's Untold Story

A SERPENT COILS around my body as I lay by the river bank. Sunlight trickles between hefty fig leaves, dappling black scales with shadow. The serpent's head is at my lips. Its split tongue flicks between my teeth and slips inside. I welcome it, choking, gagging, as the serpent slithers down my throat and into my being. Here, it moves through intestine and vein. Flesh undulates at the surface as the creature weaves between ribs. A bone snaps. Its jagged edge scrapes internal organs.

I call to the Heavens to be delivered from this agony. But God does not answer. He deplores my dealings with the serpent. My free will is oppressed.

The serpent ascends from the depths of hot bowel, pressing against heart and lungs, stealing breath during the esophageal retreat back to earth. My incisors scrape serpent skin. Scales loosen and fall to my tongue as two meters of snaking flesh exits.

I gasp for breath. Life-saving, glorious breath.

With a stabbing pain in my side, I raise hands to the clouds above, praising the Almighty, but the sunlight wanes behind thickening clouds.

God turns His back to me.

I worry not. He will not harm me, for He does not carry vengeance in His heart as I do. Vengeance is born of the earth.

At my feet, the serpent wretches. Convulsing, it spews an object from its unhinged jaw. A curved white bone coated in blood. A piece of myself, not just flesh, but bone and marrow. The power to create life lies in my hands. I'll be an equal to Eve, and to God, once and for all.

At the garden's center, Eve pores over her scrolls. Her beauty surpasses all of the garden's fruit. Black curls drape over soft shoulders, spilling to the grass where she reclines over her parchment. With a yellow feather dipped in berry's ink, she scribes her story—a history of how she and I came into existence:

In the beginning, God created the heaven and the earth...

My blood drips from the tip of the extracted bone as I approach her.

She who is God's most favorable creation. *She* who was born from the heaven's stardust and fruit of the earth. *She* who was gifted the knowledge of creation—an equal to God Himself. The scripture on those pages tells the story. It's a story I know well:

AND GOD LOVED his creation of the heaven and earth so, he wished to share its beauty with another. From the dust of the heavens and the supple fruits of the earth, he forged a woman and named her Eve. And she was perfect. She was good. An equal to God in knowledge and love.

However, Eve was bound to the earth, so she asked God why she walked alone. God assured that she was not alone, but that He was with her, in the subtle whisper of the tree's leaves and the rambling brook through the garden.

But Eve challenged God still. As the birds have each other, she too wished for a partner, for someone to share the beauty of this earth.

And so God endowed upon Eve the ability to create life. She could share the beauty of God's creations with another, but must give up immortality to do so.

With God's approval, Eve whispered to the garden serpent an arrangement. It slipped inside, coiling, twisting within her soul. From her womb and marrow, the serpent extracted a drop of her life force and delivered it to Eve's hand. In payment for his service, Eve allowed the serpent to keep a fallen yellow bird she had been tending to. She mourned the loss of life, but new life would spring forth soon.

In the soft clay of the earth, she placed her life force, blood, tears, and immortality so another may enjoy the glory of life.

She forged a man and named him Adam.

They walked together in the Garden, and God was with them in the gentle hush of the wind and in the rolling thunder before the rain...

The serpent, who only serves himself, awaits his payment; a yellow songbird, the brightest and most pleasant voice in all of the garden—Eve's favorite of God's creations. I pluck a healthy fledgling from the nest and turn it over to the slithering creature. Yellow feathers thrash in the jaws of the serpent. Its screech snaps into silence.

Emerald leaves rustle in reaction to the deal. Bruised clouds choke out the light above.

I clutch my disembodied bone in my fist and approach Eve from behind. The bloody, sharp bone twists in my palm. She can create life, but denies me the right to do the same. From over her shoulder, I read her latest scripture:

Adam is not ready. He wishes not to create for the sake of sharing God's beauty. Instead, Adam desires power. He grows impatient, and speaks often to the serpent by the river bank...

An exodus of yellow birds from the trees know my intentions. The fluttering golden wings against the gray and purple clouds bring Eve to her feet. Outstretched arms embrace their beauty.

God speaks in a rumble of thunder—a warning, perhaps.

Eve drops her scrolls to the soft grass. Her eyes widen, all-loving, all-knowing. In them, I see my creator, my mother, my love...*My inhibitor.*

I thrust the bone into her belly. She grunts, shoulders jerking forward as her delicate flesh is pierced to the core. Dear Eve stumbles into me and I lower her gently to the ground. Blood spills, soaking into the soft green grasses.

I kneel beside her, stirring the bone dagger within her gut, scraping until there is nothing recognizable left. Viscera smacks and suctions like wet clay. Eve holds my gaze as starlight fades from her eyes and is blotted out by the reflection of gray, oppressive clouds.

Yellow birds turn black as pitch. Their song becomes a mournful dirge.

I back away from her lifeless body.

What have I done?

I must act quickly. From clay, I carve a new woman. Sculpting each limb, each curve, to perfection. My rib, now blood-soaked with Eve's life force, presses into the soft sculpture.

I give of myself to make her new.

Gently, I touch my lips to my creation. Bitter, wet clay lingers on my tongue. My tears soak into her sodden form and I breathe life into a new Eve—*my* Eve. Created from my rib, she will be a compliment to myself. One who will bear *my* children. Children who will sow the earth.

My creation opens her eyes. Eyes that are unknowing, lost, devoid of God's knowledge. I wait for God to speak, to uncover my grisly truths, to punish me for what I have done. But the leaves are still. The thunder no longer carries his voice.

God is not vengeful, but he has abandoned earth. He has abandoned Man.

I am weakened now, mortal among the earth and all of God's creations.

I name her Eve, and before she can discover the remains of her predecessor, I send the new woman to explore the fruit of the garden. A raven screeches, shedding a black feather that lands in the crimson pool of my rage. I must hide the evidence.

Eve's scrolls are on the grass beside her body. Her account of the creation of life. Should my new Eve find these writings, she will abandon me just as God has.

I need to craft a story.

A lie.

I remove the pages which tell the story of Eve—God's *perfect* creation. They are buried with her body, deep in the soil, never to be seen by our descendants' eyes.

With the fallen raven feather soaked in Eve's blood, I scratch onto the scrolls a new account of Adam and Eve: God's most prized and perfect creation of *Man*.

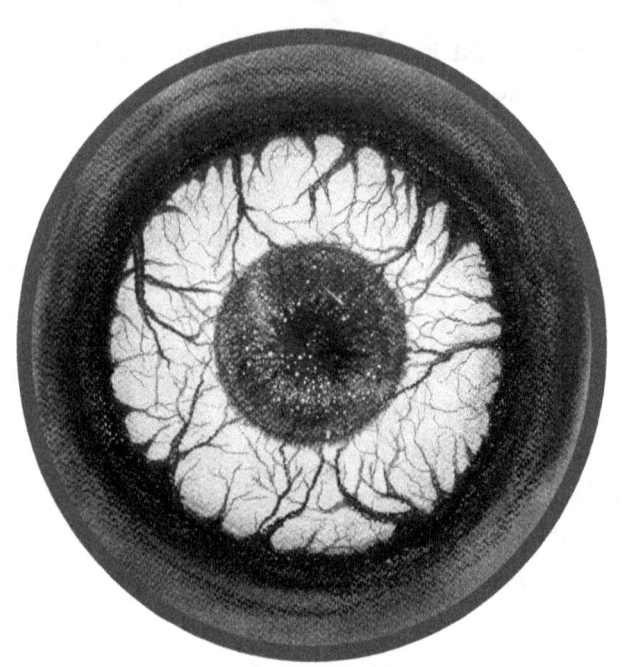

SHUTTER STOP

THE SACRED CIRCLE NATURE PRESERVE was fenced off decades ago. Deep in the heart of the state forest, most people never ventured to it. Local lore stated that those who dared capture the Sacred Circle's beauty were forever cursed—something about *Forbidden Knowledge*. Vannah didn't believe in curses, and it wasn't as if anyone would be in the middle of the forest on a cold November night to stop her.

Wire cutters snapped through the chain link fence with ease.

NO Trespassing, NO Photography, warned the small sign attached to the six-foot tall fence. Vannah had backpacked her camera gear forty-five minutes through state park wilderness to get there.

Tall white pine trees stood like cathedral columns of some vast and ancient hall. Splotches of orange sunlight spilled from the west onto a blanket of pine straw. Her phone lost its signal, but no maps or GPS were necessary to find her way from this point. As long as she walked a straight line, she'd be at the center of the five-hundred acre circle of land within ten minutes.

Vannah had read about the large open field at the preserve's center although it was damn near impossible to get any information on the place. Satellite imagery revealed a blurry patch, pixelated and unreadable. It piqued her interest even more.

A short hike through columns of trees ended and Vannah stepped into a stadium-sized meadow. The Sacred Circle. The sun had lowered behind the massive pines, soaking the field in green-gray shadow.

Her eyes lifted to the cloudless, fading blue sky as she marched through the tall grasses toward the center of the circle. The nearest city was miles away. Vast horizons created the perfect dome for observation. An astronomer's dream, the location was ideal for photographing the annual Leonid Meteor Shower.

NO Photography, they warned. She wondered who *they* were. The people who put up the signs, who started the folklore. The people who believed in nonsense. Probably hippies from the 70s. Maybe some weird pagan group. Or perhaps a native tribe, honoring ancient beliefs. Vannah meant no disrespect. She'd set up camp, take some photographs, and be out by dawn. No harm, no foul. Sometimes it's better to ask forgiveness than permission anyway.

After setting up her tent and tripod, Vanna kicked back and waited for the sky to darken. The chill of the November air bit at her nose, but as an amateur astronomer, she was no stranger to long, cold nights under the stars.

The sky blackened and the stars lit up the night. Those specks of light traveled across the galaxy to reach her. Stargazing allowed the observer a glimpse into the past at that all-knowing light from a thousand years ago. But it never felt that way for Vannah. When she sat beneath starlight, she didn't think about the past. Instead, she imagined the future. All the things that could be. The so-called *Forbidden Knowledge* was hers for the taking. Vannah chuckled under her breath.

The camera's shutter opened automatically to begin intervals of thirty-second exposures. Peak meteor time wouldn't be for hours, but she planned on imaging all night. She settled into a camp chair beneath the starry dome and let the light penetrate her soul.

A white light streaked across the sky. The camera shutter closed.

"Yes!" The odds of catching a meteor on the first shot were slim. A bright meteor so early in the evening foretold an exciting night of astrophotography.

The shutter opened for another shot. She reclined, bundled in her winter gear, a smile frozen on her face.

A deep groan came from the woods, melting her grin away.

The abysmal moan of a massive tree bending under its weight. It emanated from every direction as if the entire forest cried out on the verge of collapse. Vannah stood at the center of the field. The ground swelled, pressing against the soles of her feet.

The tripod rocked. She staggered with the moving earth to rescue her gear. With a steadying grip, she held the tripod and cut the camera's power.

The swaying of the earth stopped as suddenly as it crept in.

"What the hell?"

No photography, they warned. She pushed the lore out of her mind and considered logical explanations.

Earthquake? She lived in this area for years and never experienced one. She steadied her racing heart and regained composure. There was an explanation for everything, and if she were anywhere within range of a cell tower, she'd get online and try to find the source of the strange geologic activity. For now, there was nothing left to do but make sure her gear was okay. Using her red LED flashlight, she leveled her tripod and went to work adjusting the camera's field of view on the sky. Her finger caught on the SD card compartment cover. It was wide open, card slot empty.

"Idiot," she said. She couldn't believe she had forgotten to put it in.

A backup card took its place and she set the camera to begin intervals of exposures. She'd scan the ground for dropped items with her red light and then duck into the tent to warm up. As she backed away from the tripod, she spotted a small dark square tucked between the blades of grass—an SD card. That minor quake shouldn't have made the card fall out.

Bitter cold crept into her thin gloves and nipped at her fingers as she picked it up.

Weird.

Once inside her tent, she opened her laptop to see if either of the two pictures came out alright. She slid the card into the slot. On the laptop's screen, instead of an image of the meteor, there was a woman lying on her side, face half-buried in a bed of pine straw, eyes wide open. Slack-jawed. Vannah nearly didn't recognize herself. Blood-smeared scratches riddled her face. A thick layer of blood coated her neck.

Her gut leapt to her throat. The dark mole on her jaw and small scar over her eyebrow matched her own.

How is this possible?

A prank? Maybe her computer had been hacked.

Analyze the situation.

That's what Vannah was great at—analyzing market trends. Far better than any of her peers. Even outside of work, she analyzed everything—her relationships, her childhood. People's ridiculous belief systems. She could distance herself from emotion and irrational thoughts and analyze until the world made sense.

It's gotta be a prank.

Vannah clicked the next image. Another shot of herself appeared. In this photograph, she stood with her back against a large boulder.

At least I'm not dead in this one.

The picture exposed a gash across her left cheek, blood seeping from the wound. She appeared to be terrified, looking over her shoulder for something.

Outside, the camera shutter automatically closed and jerked her attention away from the laptop. Vannah slid her gloves on and unzipped the door. Her dim red flashlight replaced the bright white light of the computer screen. She allowed her eyes to adjust to the abyss of darkness.

She had underestimated how dark it would be in The Circle. The cloudy haze of the Milky Way stretched from horizon to horizon. Were it not for the starlight, it would be difficult to tell where the tarry black of the treetops ended and the black sky began.

The zipper screamed in the quiet of the night as she closed it behind her. As she stepped away from the tent, a faint whispering seeped into earshot.

She sucked in a sharp breath and held it to listen. Consonant-heavy staccato whispers from the direction she had hiked in. The flashlight's beam fell short onto the tips of tall grasses. The blackness beyond cloaked the whisperer.

Campground? How far can sound travel on wind? Sound carrying miles from the campground, even on a freakish wind, didn't seem likely.

Lost hikers?

The Sacred Circle protectors? The people who warned of the dangers of capturing photographs. Maybe there was something out here they didn't want people to see. The idea that someone was hiding sinister secrets out here hadn't occurred to her.

The camera shutter opened for another interval. Vannah jumped.

Another groan rumbled from the trees. The ground swelled beneath her feet. She adjusted her gait to balance. Treetops at the horizon seemed to reach inward. They stretched impossibly far overhead, choking out the light of the stars, narrowing the patch of open sky.

The hissing whispers in the trees intensified.

The camera shutter closed.

"Okay! I get the point. I'm done!" With shaking hands, she grabbed the camera and unscrewed it from the tripod.

Vannah backed against the tent as the whispers of indiscernible words closed in. Nothing made sense. She unzipped the door and scrambled inside.

The voices ceased. The groan of the trees and quaking earth relaxed. As much as she hated to admit it, she reasoned she could have been hallucinating—*but how?*

Everything can be explained.

Inside the tent, she removed her gloves. Her pulse pounded between her ears, making it difficult to focus on an explanation for the events.

The camera had taken at least two more exposures of the sky before she took it off the tripod. A shaking hand pressed the playback button to review the photographs directly on the display panel.

A dark image jumped into the two-by-three inch screen. She drew her eyes closer and adjusted the brightness. Vannah's face stared back through the window. In this photograph, she was on hands and knees, crawling through thorny branches. A skinny bent tree stump stood behind her—*no. Something else.*

Increasing the brightness of the display, and zooming on the image, exposed a pale, dirty leg. A barefoot person lurked behind, ragged dark fabric hanging to the knee. The image cut off above the person's waist.

The whispering voices returned, louder, closer. Vannah, losing all ability to find reason or rationale in what was happening, fumbled to dial the emergency function on her phone, but when she pressed the button, a loading circle appeared, rotating, rotating, rotating…

No signal, as expected.

"Come on!" she said under her breath. *Think.*

The Sacred Circle had to be the center of some strange geological activity.

The photographs still made no sense, but they had to mean something.

Forbidden Knowledge—they claimed. A pressure built in her head as she tried to piece it together.

Knowledge of what? Her death?

It doesn't make sense.

Vannah dug her knife from her backpack. In all the years camping and late-night stargazing, she'd never felt the need to pull the six-inch blade from its sheath. "Back off, assholes! I'm armed."

The whispers encroached like a suffocating static. No distinct words, just heavy consonants clicking and hissing in the night.

"I'll delete the images. All of them! I'm sorry!"

With the abrupt silence of clicking off a television, the voices stopped.

Vannah set her knife aside and held the camera in both hands. She pressed delete. "I deleted it!"

The next photo appeared on the screen. A glare of red-orange—the color of her tent walls. In this picture, Vannah sat inside the tent with her hand cupped over her mouth as she stared into the screen of her Canon.

This is now.

Upon seeing herself in this present moment, she drew her hand to her mouth in shock. Someone behind her, with her in the tent, had to have taken the photo. Fear ran its fingernail along Vannah's spine. Her pulse hammered between her ears as she trapped a breath in her throat. With the stiffness of a corpse, she slowly turned to look over her shoulder.

Alone.

She released her breath. Uncontrollable vibrations rattled through her bones, chattering her teeth. Tears stung her eyes.

Vannah dropped the camera to the floor and snatched up her knife.

They wanted her out and she couldn't get the tent open fast enough. The zipper caught on the fabric. Vannah grunted and sliced through the material with her blade.

She charged out, feet tripping over the ragged tent wall. The blackness swallowed her up into its dispiteous dark. She swung her knife into the nothing, sprinting through pitch black toward the woods, keeping her mind to head in the direction she hiked in.

Maybe she could get away unseen or unheard. Hoping whoever or whatever was out there wouldn't see her escaping, she left her red light tucked in her coat pocket. After tripping twice, she slowed her pace and quieted her frantic emotions.

Keep your head. Find your way out.

If she went the way she came in, following a straight path through the trees, she would find her way to the fence. The columns of tree trunks drew near, growing taller, leaning in as she slipped out of the open field of The Sacred Circle and into the surrounding pine forest. It was a half-mile to the fence—to the safety of the state park.

The spacing between the trees narrowed. Twigs snagged her pant legs. Her hands explored the black path ahead, but landed onto a patch of thick briars. She must've gone the wrong way, because this path was clear on the hike in. A brief glimpse with her flashlight exposed the thick brush obstructing her way.

"Stop." A sharp-tongued voice said from behind.

Vannah shrieked and dove to the ground. Knife in hand, she crawled beneath the briars. Her hands sank into a thick bed of pine straw as she pulled herself through. Whip-thin boughs slapped her cheeks.

Footsteps and whispers loomed behind. She dug her light from her pocket and aimed it over her shoulder. Standing behind her, beyond the thick tangles of brush, stood a dirty, pale leg, illuminated in her beam of red light. It was the exact image of the photograph she had seen earlier. But there was nobody in front of her taking pictures—nobody she could see.

Vannah's scream caught in her throat as she struggled to tear out of the brush. She stood too soon. Thorns ripped open the flesh of her left cheek.

She ran, red light pumping through the black void between the pines. She slashed her blade through the air. The sounds of her footfalls and hyperventilating were a siren in the night, surely alerting the whisperers of her location. She needed to get control.

Instead, with no time to assess her situation, she ran, dodging pine trees, boulders, and roots as they materialized from the deathly black.

The whispers fell farther behind.

Now. She ducked behind a boulder and shut off her light. Tears poured into the wound on her left cheek, stinging. Sweat dripped down her neck and soaked into her shirt. Her panting was so severe she grew faint trying to quiet herself.

As she stood against the boulder, terrified, she realized it was a reenactment of the image she'd seen earlier.

This is a psychological trick.

They're just people. Sick people. Clutching the blade, she clenched her jaw and flared her nostrils like a bull, ready to fight.

Slow deep breaths. Think.

She peered beyond the boulder and caught a glimpse of a pale square, seeming to float between the trees. A flick of her light exposed it as the back of a sign hanging from a chain link fence. A sign she was certain would read: *NO Trespassing, NO Photography.*

The odds that she found her way back to the exact spot she had cut the fence were slim. There was no time to seek out the hole she'd cut. She'd need to climb over.

Vannah turned her head, exposing an ear to listen for voices. Her heart hammered against her ribs so hard she wanted to vomit.

Go.

She pushed off the boulder and ran.

"Stop," a gravelly voice said to her right. It vibrated through the ground and shuddered in her joints.

Vanna screamed. Her blade swung toward the whisperer, but it sliced through nothing but darkness.

Run!

A root caught her foot as she twisted to get away. Vannah lost her footing. She thrust her arms out to take the impact of the fall.

The sting of her own blade penetrated her neck.

With her left arm trapped beneath the weight of her body, Vannah lay on her side. Fingers still wrapped around the knife handle, she eased the blade from her throat and gagged as blood filled the void left behind. Her fingers lost strength and released their grip. Radiant heat flowed out of her and draped over the cold sweat of her neck like a warm scarf.

The whispers receded into the forest. The pines leaned as Vanna's vision tunneled. With a collective sigh, the trees rested into their places as all light and reason faded into darkness. Through the branches of the pine canopy, a star shone. It winked from a thousand years ago—or maybe from a thousand years in the future—mocking Vanna's trespasses as she suffocated on the blood of her forbidden knowledge.

FLICKER

Kira

KIRA CORBIN HAD BEEN KICKED OUT of after-school daycare for destroying the communal dollhouse. All the kids had been fighting over it. Kira covered her ears and screamed for them to stop. Next thing she knew, the painted, cardboard house was squashed flat and all the kids cried. Third grade did not get off to a good start. Despite the incident being a big, fat accident, her mom thought it best to move even farther away from dad and start fresh.

Mom said if Kira weren't so close to her dad, maybe she wouldn't be breaking down dollhouses whenever she got mad. But she couldn't help how she felt. Sometimes those emotions took over and parts of her dad came through.

Kira turned her bedroom's overhead light on and off. When she did it really fast, it looked spooky, like a haunted house.

"Kira!" her mom said from down the hall. "What's up with the lights?"

"Nothing. I'm just playing with them." She flopped on her bed in her llama pajamas.

Her mom entered the room and joined her on the bed. "Like your dad?"

Dad moved out of the house when she was six and visits became scarce after that, even though they lived only twenty minutes apart. Then, last week, they moved out of the city and into a little ranch home miles away. It took forty-five minutes to get to her dad now.

Kira shrugged. "I miss him."

"I know." Her mom pulled her in for a hug. "I'm sorry things are like this."

The light flickered. Kira lifted her eyes to the ceiling. A sharp pain stabbed Kira in the nose. She grabbed at the bridge, eyes watering.

"What's wrong?" Her mom fawned over her.

Three stuffed animals fell from her shelf onto the floor.

Mom jolted upright. "Kira, what's happening?"

"I don't know."

"Is it him?" her mom asked.

Sometimes when she and her dad thought of each other at the same time, things would happen. Stuff would move, lights would flicker, or she'd feel his thoughts. Sometimes things would break if she was upset. That was dad's energy coming through to help.

She hopped off her bed to pick up her stuffies and placed them back on the shelf. Piggy stayed pressed against her heart.

The pain in her nose went away and sadness took its place. It filled her so much she felt like she would crack open from the inside.

"I'm sorry, Kira. I thought distance would help."

She tried to put on a smile for her mom. "That's okay. I get to say 'good night' to dad every night."

"You do?"

"Mhmm. I say, 'Good night, Daddy,' and then all the way from the city, he says, 'Goodnight, my light.'"

Kira's bones ached from her dad's sorrow.

"He calls you his light because his world is so dark." Mom's eyes went watery again. They did that whenever Kira talked about her dad. "He loves you so much. He's a good man who had bad things happen to him, that's all."

"I know."

Her mom wiped the corners of her eyes.

Kira hated it when Mom cried, so she changed the subject. "The neighbors have pigs!" She wiggled her stuffed piggy. "*Real* pigs."

"I met them a few days ago. Maybe they'll let you see their pigs."

"Really?"

"Maybe. I had a long chat with the wife. We really hit it off. Her name's Jessica."

Jessica

Jessica smacked Dante across the cheek with the back of her hand. "You're a drunken piece of shit, aren't you?"

Duct tape sealed his mouth shut. The intoxicated man slumped in his seat, eyes unable to lock on any one thing. His sedative wore thin.

Earlier, Jessica had waited for Dante outside of a bar in Syracuse—exactly where the new neighbor Sherrie said he spent his time nowadays. She pulled right up and offered the staggering drunk a ride. He hopped in like a she was driving a goddamned free-candy van. Jessica popped him with a syringe of Ketamine and drove forty-five minutes back home. From the garage, she walked him down to the basement where she sat him in a chair against a support beam and tied his hands behind his back. A rope bound his feet. Beneath him laid a sheet of painter's plastic.

Dante's eyes rolled around and then steadied on her.

"There you are," she said, leaning closer to allow him to focus.

Watching her victims realize they're trapped was Jessica's favorite part. Their eyes went from confused to panic.

Heavy footsteps above signaled her husband Mario's return. Nervous energy coursed through her as he crossed the kitchen.

Dante struggled within his binds and screamed through the duct tape.

"Shhh!" Jessica pulled the cord to the overhead light and the cellar went black.

"Jessica?" Mario's voice seeped through the kitchen floor.

The cellar door opened and Mario came down the stairs. He stopped at the bottom of the steps, his large frame silhouetted against the light at the top of the stairway.

She pulled the cord to the light. "Surprise!"

Dante sat in a rocking pool of yellow light as the bulb swayed over his head.

"Jesus, Jessica!" Mario said.

"Don't get upset." She held her palms up.

"Who the hell is that?"

"It's *him*. The guy the new neighbor told me about. The drunk that choked her in her sleep." Jessica's upper lip curled with disgust.

Dante murmured urgently through the duct tape.

She got in his face. "You don't get to talk!"

"What did you do?" Mario put his hands on top of his head.

"I had to. For her. And for *you*. It's been a long time since you've had a catch." Her words met a blank stare and her breath hitched in anticipation of Mario's reaction.

He closed in on her and shook his head. "What am I going to do with you?"

Dante

Dante cringed as the couple kissed in front of him. If only his mind were sharp, he'd be able to get out of this mess without a problem. However, these last few years he had made it a point to keep himself intoxicated as much as possible.

The fog of the sedation dissipated, but not enough to see through it yet. With each passing minute, the haze would thin, and he'd be able to focus on undoing his binds. First, he concentrated on the light above. It swayed, making him nauseous.

You are in control. Dante settled his thoughts and honed in on the light. It clicked off. Blackness draped the cellar.

"Damn it!" Jessica said.

Pulling in the scant amount of energy he could, he worked at the duct tape over his mouth. His mind peeled it away from the corner of his lips.

The light snapped back on and Mario's large frame hovered over him, hanging onto the string.

Jessica smoothed the duct tape back over his lips. He craned his neck away from her, again focusing his attention on the tape.

The light flickered. Dante's mind went fuzzy. Normally, he could send people flying across the room if he needed to. He could launch objects through the air. But not when he was under the influence. The drug-induced haze stifled his attempt to remove the duct tape, but he pushed through it. Using all his strength, he willed the tape to rip off his face and fall to the floor.

Jessica gasped. "What the hell?"

"You don't want to mess with me," Dante said.

"How'd he get the tape off, Mario?" Jessica asked.

"You probably didn't stick it on right."

"There's only one way to stick it!"

Scanning the basement for a weapon, Dante found shelves of paint cans and old rusted tools. A hammer. Maybe he could fling it at Mario's head. He focused his energy on his binds, but he couldn't get them loose. "I'm warning you," he bluffed and flickered the bulb again.

Mario squared his shoulders and moved closer. "What are you going to do, little man?" He delivered a swift jab. Dante's nose snapped. His head felt like it cracked in half from the blow. Blood poured from his nostrils. He thought of his beautiful daughter and hoped she didn't sense what was happening. The shelves lining the cellar walls rattled.

The hammer fell from the shelf to the floor.

"What was that?" Jessica jumped. "Mario, something weird's going on."

Dante's vision blurred. "I don't know who you people think you are..."

Jessica pulled a canvas bag from the shelf and set it on a wooden tray table. "We're the people that make sure abusive pricks like you don't go on hurting other people."

"That's not how it is—"

"We take matters into our own hands." Jessica unfolded the flaps of the bag to reveal neatly situated rows of knives and saws."

Mario stood back, arms crossed.

"What do you want from me?"

"We want your wife and daughter to be free of you." Jessica's words sliced through his heart.

Dante wanted his family to be free of him too. That's all he wanted—for Sherrie and Kira to live a happy life. Dante flexed his wrists, fighting against the binds. *Focus, you idiot.* If he couldn't get his mind under control, he'd die. He took a steadying breath. Maybe dying wouldn't be so bad. He'd never have to worry about accidentally killing them in their sleep. After Afghanistan, when the PTSD started, Dante's abilities went haywire. Nightmares sent books flying from shelves and knives from drawers. One night, Dante dreamt about strangling an insurgent. His nightmare oozed into reality and he woke with his hands around Sherrie's neck. His mind was too dangerous to be around his family, so he drank it into submission.

The drinking led to other problems, which led to their separation. Sweet Sherrie didn't want him to leave, but he insisted for the safety of his daughter. They deserved so much more than he could give them.

He should've gotten control of his life sooner, but he sought help too late. The sting of tears burned behind his lids. He fought the quiver in his chin. Dante wished his loves a farewell in his mind. His bones ached from the sorrow.

"Aww…" Jessica tilted her head then smacked him across the face. "You don't get to cry! You tried to kill your wife."

"No," Dante whispered. "It's the PTSD. A night terror gone wrong."

Jessica huffed. "Some women don't have what it takes to stand up to a toxic man."

Mario remained silent by the stairs as Jessica did all the talking.

"But not me. I stand up for the women who can't stand up for themselves. She nodded to Mario. "You know how Mario and I met?" Jessica dragged a stool in front of Dante and sat face to face.

"I don't care." Blood dripped from his nose into his mouth. He turned his head and spit it out onto the plastic. *Focus on the ropes.* He made eye contact with Jessica as she rested her pale chin on her fist.

"We had just started dating, Mario and me."

Mario pulled a gleaming blade from the bag and showcased it in the light.

If Dante focused, maybe he could knock Mario out with something from the shelves.

Jessica smiled. "I was at my place and I had a catch. A scrappy little man. The pervert thought he'd feel me up at the bar and try to follow me home." She shrugged. "So I let him."

Dante allowed her to tell the story. Her words became background noise while he focused on the paint cans, measured the weight in his mind. The energy was there, behind the fog in his head, in the sludge of his slow-pumping blood. He just had to clear his mind.

"I had my apartment covered in plastic like this," Jessica said, gesturing to the floor. "My blades were set. I sliced open his throat and let it pour into a bucket like tap water, when…" She smacked her knee. "Mario walks in and says, 'Hey baby, hope you don't mind I made myself a key.'"

Mario gave her a smirk and raised an eyebrow. "What are the odds?"

"I thought you'd call the cops or run, but no. You stayed and helped me finish the job. *That's* love."

Dante pulled his attention from the paint can. "So, you found another psycho just like you?"

"It's not psycho to want the world to be a better place." Jessica's eyes squinted.

"So he made a key to get into your place and kill you, but he found you in the middle of killing someone else? Yeah, romantic."

"No!" Jessica said. She looked to Mario and shook her head. "No."

Dante pulled his attention inward. *Stop getting distracted.*

"I think it's time to gag this guy again, babe." Mario handed her the roll of duct tape.

Jessica ripped off a strip and slapped it over Dante's mouth. "God, it was so cathartic. The blood of that pervert pouring into the bucket while we realized we were meant for each other..." She looked toward Mario and shivered.

Dante felt a clearing in his head and finally forced the paint can from the shelf. It hurtled through the air and smacked into Mario's head. The linebacker of a man stumbled forward, but it didn't knock him out. Another paint can to his head sent him to his knees.

Dante, with everything he had in him, sent the cans and tools from the shelves. The shelving rattled. The light sputtered. His binds loosened, but not enough to pull free yet.

"What's going on?" Jessica grabbed onto Mario as he stood up.

Dante stared intently at his targets as they flinched and held up hands to block the rusted cans.

"It's him," Jessica said. "He's doing it somehow."

Mario charged Dante and ripped off the duct tape. "What's happening, freak?"

"*I'm* the freak?" Dante let out a nervous laugh.

Jessica pulled a syringe from the bag and lunged toward him.

He sent a hammer through the air and it whacked Jessica in the back of the head. She dropped.

Dante used up his energy too quickly. The haze overwhelmed him. He couldn't stay focused long enough to continue. He worked at his hands and pulled his left arm free.

Mario took the syringe from Jessica and flew at Dante. Before Dante could set his other hand loose, Mario plunged the syringe into Dante's thigh. A sting and burning sensation flooded his muscle.

The cinderblock walls of the cellar bowed inward, as if the entire house took a deep breath. Walls cracked and moaned while everyone in the room froze in place. Dante had never been able to do *that* before. *Focus.* He held onto that emotion. The anger and fear—the need to survive. The need to see Kira again…

"Mario?" Jessica's voice trembled.

Before Mario could back away, Dante swung a left hook into his jaw. The guy barely flinched then pinned Dante's arm down. His teeth were bared as he fought Dante to hold still.

The drugs overcame him. The paint cans fell still. The fissures in the wall crumbled under the weight of the home while the cinderblocks relaxed and sat back into their normal state.

Dante's neck struggled to hold his heavy head. It would finally be over. His family would be free of him.

"Goodnight, my light," Dante whispered.

Kira

Deep inside Kira's bones, her dad's sorrow metastasized. Her heart raced and a trickle of sweat rolled down her brow. Dad was scared.

Another war nightmare? She closed her eyes and tried to wake him up, but it was different this time. Dad wasn't asleep. Dread and terror trudged through her blood and filled every part of her body. Her skin prickled. Her wrists went achy and sore. Kira's lips were raw and burning.

The lights flickered as Kira's breaths became quick and short.

"Kira, stop messing with the lights!" Mom said from down the hall.

She eked out an "Okay." But it wasn't her this time.

"*You* are in control of *you*." Dad used to say. Kira took a deep breath and reined in all that runaway fear. Dad would say, "When your thoughts go dark, it's up to you to bring them into the light."

Kira sensed her dad in that darkness, but he wouldn't come back into the light. His thoughts were getting darker and scarier. He needed help.

She grabbed a pair of shoes and snuck down the hallway. With ninja stealth, Kira slipped outside. Her face ached and tears stung her eyes as she ran down the country road. Twilight's light faded, turning the fields and distant trees into a blue-gray blur—a backdrop for the fireflies skimming across the tips of tall weeds.

Something pulled at her, a hook in her gut reeling her out of her house and toward her dad's cries. It didn't make sense to be running down the road. She couldn't run all the way to the city, but she didn't have much control over her body. She passed in front of the neighbor's place. The two-story farmhouse sat back from the road, dark and cold.

Kira's gut flip-flopped, and the aching and sadness shrieked in her marrow. Her vision tunneled. The blue-gray twilight world warped in, fireflies and all, as if it would cave in on her.

Kira, being the singular point where all matter and emotions would fall into her and crush her.

From inside those heart cavities where muscles pulse and blood chugs like a train, her dad's voice emerged. "Goodnight, my light."

His light burrowed out of her heart—a stabbing pain that brought her to her knees.

The lights in the farmhouse basement windows flickered. The ache in her wrists, lips, and cheeks faded. As her dad's sadness dissipated, she should have felt relief, but instead an emptiness replaced the pain.

"Dad?" she whispered into the void.

He didn't respond.

The neighbor's basement lights went steady as Dad's cries fell silent in her heart.

"Dad?" She drew closer to the neighbor's house, hugging Piggy to her chest.

The house towered like an old Victorian haunted mansion. It didn't look so creepy in the daytime, but with the colors fading in the darkness, she couldn't tell where windows began and ended, whether curtains were open or shut. Except for that one basement window with the light on.

"Dad?" Kira spoke up, unsure if her voice even made it to the house.

She drew closer to peek inside, but as she neared, the light flicked off and went blacker than tar.

"Dad?" she said again. She tried to think of him, hoping to meet his thoughts and make him feel better, but there was nothing left to feel. Like he disappeared from everywhere, and all that was left was a weird *not-dad* kind of energy.

A snorting sound from around the back of the house drew her thoughts away. She ran across the yard, past the piles of brush and the wood piles. In a pen not much bigger than her room, there were three enormous pigs. They had to be hundreds of pounds each.

Kira smiled and ran up to the fence lined with chicken wire. She poked her fingers through the wire mesh and peeked inside. Two of the pigs slept, but one met Kira at the fence. His whiskery snout tickled her fingertips. His snout went back to the mud, exploring every footprint crater. She made her own fingertip craters in the mud at the fence's edge. Knuckle-deep in the cold goo, her pointer brushed against something smooth and hard. She pinched the pebble-sized thing between her fingers, pulled it out, and wiped it on her llama PJ pants.

A tooth.

"Does this belong to you?" she asked the pig. She held the large molar up to the rising moonlight.

Uh-oh. Dad's sadness and bad feelings went away, and she couldn't be found sneaking around the neighbor's house at night. They might think she was trying to steal something. She'd been gone a long time and mom would be mad if she knew she left the house without telling her. Kira popped up and sprinted across the field, toward the line of pines that separated their properties. She bolted through, sprinting as fast as she could to get back before mom checked on her.

Mario

As soon as Dante Corbin went limp from the Ketamine injection, Mario picked up the blade and skewered his heart clean through. The dangling bulb stopped flickering and glowed steady.

Jessica sat on the steps, hugging her arms tight to her body. "What the hell just happened?"

"I don't know." Mario cleaned the blade on a paper towel, sprayed it with the cleanser, and polished it spotless. It was a ritual he used to enjoy as much as the killing, but with Jessica mucking everything up lately, there was little left to find pleasure in.

Jessica ran her fingers along the cracks in the walls. "How did he do that?"

"I don't know."

"How is that poss—"

"I don't know!" Mario clenched his teeth and slammed the knife down on the table. He pulled out the bone saw and tried to refrain from fulfilling the fantasy of slicing open his wife's head. "It's over."

"Dad?" A small voice said from outside.

Mario whipped his head to Jessica who had jumped to her feet. He grabbed the cord to the light and pulled. The basement went black.

Jessica's silhouette drew toward the window. Her nervous breaths cut through the darkness. Mario's eyes adjusted to the inky black. A whisper of light marked the edges of the body slumped in the chair. The body of a man she had no business bringing home.

"It's his kid," Jessica said.

"Christ, Jessica." Mario clenched his fingers around the handle of the bone saw.

"This is *my* fault?"

"Think about it. This is *all* your fault. It's sloppy. The middle of the day. You bring him back to our house so soon after the last one."

"Dad?" The kid's voice drew closer.

Mario pulled Jessica away from the window and covered her mouth. He should've slit her throat for being so reckless.

Jessica pulled away from him. "I'm sorry." Her whispers were sharp, loud. "You haven't had a catch in so long, I thought I'd give you one."

Mario leaned closer and kept a steady tone. "You're getting too hungry and it's going to cost us."

"It was for *you*."

"That's a lie." Mario's nostrils flared. He eased one eye to the edge of the window. "The kid's gone."

Jessica yanked away from him and ran upstairs.

"Jessica," Mario called after her.

She didn't stop. He set down his bone saw and pulled out a new syringe. From the zippered compartment of the bag, he drew the bottle of Ketamine, then ran to the top of the stairs and turned on the bathroom light. The amber bottle, held to the light, revealed droplets clinging to the insides. The contents had been emptied. His trust in Jessica unraveled with each passing second.

"Turn that light off," Jessica said peering out the foyer window.

"Where's all the Ketamine?" he asked.

Her eyes darted to his hand and then back to the front window. "Don't worry about that. Where's the kid?"

Jessica pushed by him toward the kitchen and leaned over the sink to look out back. "Where'd she go? How'd she know he was here?"

Mario let his anger seethe to the surface, bubbling and blistering and ready to explode, then pulled it back inside where he could bottle it up for a more appropriate time. He had a body to dispose of first.

"I see her! Jessica whipped around with bulging eyes. She pulled a carving knife from the butcher's block. The shrill sound of the blade unsheathing pierced the silence. Jessica flung open the back door and sprinted after the little girl.

"Shit." Mario bolted out the door behind her.

The girl in pajamas ran toward her house. Jessica's long legs carried her across the field with the speed and precision of a wild cat. The blade of the knife blinked in the moonlight as her arms pumped. The girl's short stride took her through the line of trees separating the properties. There was no way that kid would outrun her. Mario wanted to call to Jessica to stop her, but he feared alerting the girl to their pursuit. She was far enough ahead that maybe she hadn't noticed Jessica closing in yet.

Mario pumped his legs as fast as he could. *Please, don't kill her.*

He was only a few feet away. They neared the tree line. He focused on Jessica's pace, the pattern of her footfalls, and matched it. They made it to the shadows of the trees, and Mario reached for Jessica. He grabbed her mane of blonde hair and yanked her to the ground.

Jessica let out a grunt and they both tumbled and rolled like they had leapt from a high-speed train. Jessica scrambled on top of him. She held the knife to his throat. "You son of a bitch!"

"Shhh!" Mario said, nodding his head toward the girl who had made it to her driveway.

"What's wrong with you?" Jessica's hand trembled. Her voice quaked. She pushed the blade closer to his neck.

"If you take her down here, there'll be evidence. Footprints. Blood."

"What if she tells?"

"She didn't *see* anything," Mario said.

"She was calling 'Dad.' She knows he's there."

Mario gave a gentle nudge to the handle of the knife. Jessica pulled back and sat on her knees, clutching that knife like a lifeline.

Mario got to his feet and dusted off his knees. "What are you going to do? Kill a kid?"

"I don't know. If I have to. I'll do anything to protect us."

"I know." Mario edged closer and put a hand on her shoulder. He locked eyes to win back her trust. "You have to ease up on the catches for a while."

"I was careful. Nobody saw me."

"*Think*. It was the middle of the day," Mario said. "How can you be sure?"

"You don't trust me?"

"I don't know anymore, Jessica. Where's the Ketamine? How many catches have you had behind my back? Is that why the pigs haven't been eating? How much are you feeding them?" Each question led to another and Mario had to quiet himself before he asked a question that angered her.

Jessica shook her head and crossed her arms. "Well, you haven't been interested lately."

"I don't need it like you do. I can control it. And when I do give in to the temptation, it's someone that really makes me sick. Someone that *deserves* it." Mario raked his fingers through his hair so tight, he pulled at the roots, wanting to rip it all out and shove it down her throat. That bubbling rage rattled against his chest. "You're hunting down drunks and little kids." The words slipped through his lips, steeped with spite. Mario leaned against a pine tree to calm down.

Jessica's shoulders dropped. "People who deserve it? Like me?"

"What are you talking about?"

"That night when we were dating, you made a key and came over. You were going to kill *me*. Why? Why did I *deserve* it?"

Mario's heart stuttered.

"And don't pretend you weren't going to. You're insulting my intelligence. I've played along long enough. It's time for you to tell me. If you only like to kill really bad people, what was it about me?"

"I knew you were killing people, and I figured I'd take it upon myself to bring you down. But I didn't know that the men you had killed were so awful. I didn't know you that well. I was young." Mario was impressed with his answer. He felt a smug smile grow inside his heart with his cunning lies. "Then I saw you there, so beautiful against that backdrop of death— that backdrop that so many times I had to endure alone—that I couldn't take your life. I *needed* your life, alongside mine."

Jessica turned her head away and the corner of her mouth twitched like she was refraining from smiling.

It worked. "I love you Jessica. I love what we have." Mario drew in closer and reached for her hand. "But I'd hate to see it jeopardized by doing too much too fast."

"But what about *her*?" She nodded toward the house.

"We take care of his body as usual."

"And if she tells her mom something and the police come knocking tonight?"

"Just in case," he said to quell her paranoia, "we'll lay low tonight. We can't be downstairs running the saw or out back running parts through the chipper. He goes in deep freeze for the night."

"But if they come—"

"If they come, these small-town cops aren't going to procure a warrant tonight." Mario said. "Tomorrow, after we're sure the neighbor isn't onto us, we'll work on the disposal. If they *are* onto us, we load him in the car and dump him somewhere as a last resort."

"Maybe we should just dump him somewhere tonight," Jessica said.

"Not without planning. This is how people get caught. A body dump requires research."

Jessica shifted her weight from side to side.

"But then, when it's all over, we have to lay low for a while. No more catches."

"No more catches." Jessica wrapped her arms around his neck. The unforgiving steel of the carving knife rested against his shoulder.

Mario's loving and reasonable façade would crack under the pressure of his rising rage if he didn't get rid of Jessica soon.

Jessica

Dante Corbin had scared the hell out of Jessica and she spent the night haunted by the idea that he would somehow get his revenge as a ghost. She didn't think she believed in ghosts, but she didn't believe in telekinesis either. She woke frequently throughout the night. In her dream, the walls crumbled in on her like they had in the basement, but this time they kept closing in and she couldn't escape their suffocating, crushing grasp.

Jessica and Mario didn't speak much in the morning. He went to work at the insurance agency while she headed to the veterinary hospital. Mario had texted that he'd be late, so she had until eight o'clock to get the job done. It wasn't much time, but if she cut out of work early, she could manage.

She nabbed a few more milliliters of pentobarbital—euthanasia solution—to add to her collection at home. When logged properly, she could take a little here and there and it would look legit in the book. She really outsmarted the system when she unpacked the shipment of Ketamine a few months ago and reported one bottle short. Her boss never blinked an eye because Jessica was the one who unpacked it—their most reliable employee.

It pissed her off when Mario told her to "think," as if she were some idiot without a plan. Her plan was solid. She claimed she wasn't feeling well and her boss let her go home. That body in the freezer, fully intact, ate away at her thoughts. It called for her to come cut it up before someone found it. To grind the pieces in the chipper and feed him to the pigs. It had to be done soon, before that kid started snooping around for her daddy again. First, she'd get her hands on that girl—and her mom. All three could be disposed of together. *One big clean up.*

Still in her scrubs, she threw some spaghetti on the stove and pulled the garlic bread from the freezer. As dinner cooked, she transferred her Euthasol into two syringes and tucked them into her scrub pockets.

Sherrie

Sherrie's daughter was quiet on the drive back from school. She worried about Kira. That's all she did lately. Worried about whether she could be a single mom. Worried about whether Kira would turn out okay. Worried whether this connection she had with her father would turn into something more. If Kira ever had Dante's abilities, would it break her the way it did Dante? He loved that little girl and made the ultimate sacrifice by distancing himself.

"How was school today?" Sherrie asked.

"Okay." Kira's gaze was fixed out the window.

"You've been a little off today."

"I can't feel him. I think there's something wrong."

Sherrie held her breath. As much as she tried to get used to it, she still found it eerie that Kira knew things about her dad. "I talked to him the other day and he promised to get help." Though, Sherrie wasn't sure how any traditional rehab could help a man like Dante.

"Is that why he was sad last night?" Kira asked.

"He was sad?"

"And scared."

Tears bit at Sherrie's eyes, but she forced them back. "He'll be okay."

"I don't think I'll ever see him again."

"Well, he wants to see you."

"He doesn't *want* anything now."

"What do you mean?" Sherrie glanced back in the mirror.

"I don't know."

As they passed by the neighbor's house, Jessica stood on her front porch waving.

"Maybe we can go see those pigs," Sherrie said, trying to cheer up her daughter.

"Okay." Her voice was flat. All the light that usually beamed from her daughter had dulled into a wash of gray.

A few days ago, she had glass of wine with Jessica on the porch and she got a little too talkative about Dante and his PTSD. She regretted it now and wished she hadn't said anything. Wine has a way of peeling away that barrier from her mouth and she can't help what comes out.

"Hi, Sherrie!" Jessica said, walking up the driveway.

Sherrie waved.

Kira went up the porch steps with her backpack flung over one shoulder.

Jessica wore a pair of blue scrubs. Her hands were tucked in the deep front pockets of her top.

"I got off work early and made spaghetti. Now Mario is coming home late and I have way too much food. Would you and your daughter like to come over for dinner?"

Kira stood on the steps and stared into the direction of Jessica's house. Seeing her child so zombie-like broke Sherrie's heart.

"I think I'm going to pass," Sherrie said, then lowered her voice to a whisper. "Something's wrong. I'm going to spend some time with her."

Kira watched from the front door as they talked in the driveway.

Jessica's smile faded. "I'm sorry. I hope she feels better. I just thought a little company would be nice. I get so lonely when I'm in that big house by myself."

"We can go to dinner." Kira's small voice was laced with a bit of emotion. Sherrie had a hard time reading her daughter, and envied Dante for his connection with her.

Jessica smiled. "Kira says it's fine." She nudged Sherrie with an elbow. "Come on. Don't make me drink alone."

"Okay," Sherrie said. "Can she see the pigs?"

Jessica looked back toward her house. "The pigs?"

"Kira likes pigs."

"Yeah, absolutely. I'll show her the pigs." Jessica said. "Dinner's at five."

Jessica

With the syringes tucked into her scrub top pocket, Jessica sat at the dinner table with Sherrie and Kira. She kept up conversation about work and the weather while Kira sat oddly still and quiet. If Mario believed that kid didn't know what happened to her father, then he was the one that needed to *think*.

"Eat your food," Sherrie said.

Kira broke her trance and put her hands in her lap. "I'm not really hungry."

The light flickered for a second. *Dante*—Jessica thought.

Sherrie's eyes raised. Did the wife expect Dante was here? She had to know about his strange powers. His body had to go.

Jessica eyed the light fixture. Her words caught in her throat. "I've got an electrician coming next week to look at that," she said with forced nonchalance.

"Kira," Sherrie leaned in close to her daughter. "Are you all right? Aren't you going to eat?"

"That's okay," Jessica said, eyeing the kid.

The kid's eyes shifted away. "Can I use your bathroom?"

"Of course," Jessica said. "Just around the corner, in the hall. Door on the left."

Kira left the table.

Sherrie whispered, "She's acting really strange lately. I don't mean to be rude, but I need to take her home."

Jessica stood. "I understand. Finish your wine. I'll get you some to-go containers."

As Jessica rounded the corner into the short hall that led to the kitchen, Kira stood in the doorway of the basement. Jessica slid her hand into her pocket to unsheathe the needle from its cap.

This was her chance. Muzzle the kid, drag her to the basement. One stab to the heart with the syringe and it'd be a quick, almost painless death.

Light from the basement flicked on, illuminating Kira's face.

Jessica closed in. Kira's arms were stiff by her sides as she stood over the basement stairs with an aura of knowing.

"Done in the bathroom, Kira?" Sherrie's voice came from behind.

Jessica released the syringe in her pocket, then closed the cellar door. "Wrong door, sweetie. Bathroom is behind you." *That won't work.* "Actually, I forgot; the plumbing for this bathroom has been tricky. Use the one upstairs?"

Kira nodded, then droned upstairs, unresponsive.

Sherrie released a big breath and pulled a sip of wine from her glass.

"It's a labyrinth up there," Jessica said. "Let me make sure she finds it."

She followed Kira, leaving Sherrie in the dining room. Her hand manipulated the cap of the syringe in her pocket as she stalked up the steps toward her next catch.

Mario

Mario drove home from work early to head off Jessica, who wasn't due home until six o'clock. Five years ago, when Mario had found her bleeding out the guy from the bar, he was weak. A momentary lapse in judgment made him believe he had a shot at a normal life. One with a family. But Jessica hungered for the kill more than he ever did. He had to talk her out of countless catches. Over the past several months, she had gotten out of control. Sloppy. If he didn't stop her soon, he'd be going down for the murders with her. Worse, she'd be killing people she had no right to kill.

He pulled into his driveway and packed his humanity into that deep dark pocket where he kept his rage. There was no place for either before a catch. With the Ketamine stash diminished, he'd have to take Jessica down without drugs. She was small enough to manage.

At five thirty, the house was lit like a jack-o-lantern. Jessica's car was parked in the garage—home early.

"Shit." Mario parked in the driveway. The scent of Italian food hit him as he walked in the foyer. In the dining room to his right, his neighbor Sherrie stood alone with a glass of red.

"Hi," she said.

Mario nodded.

"Jessica's upstairs," Sherrie said. "She's showing my daughter the way to the bathroom."

Mario sprinted up the steps. He flung open the master bedroom door to see Jessica standing beside the closed bathroom door with her hand behind her back.

"Where's the kid?" Mario asked.

"Bathroom."

"Did you do it?" Mario didn't want to know the answer. He couldn't fathom the rage he'd have if Jessica went through with slaughtering a child.

"Not yet." Jessica pulled her hand from behind her back and slid a syringe into her pocket. He immediately recognized the signature pink color of euthanasia solution.

"Jesus, Jessica."

The small knife strapped to his arm beneath his sleeve called for him to end her. He crossed his arms and slid his hand up his bicep.

"Don't," Jessica said, yanking the uncapped syringe from her pocket.

"Is everything okay up there?" Sherrie called from the bottom of the stairs.

The bathroom door opened and Kira stood in the doorway, innocent and frail. Her doe eyes looked to Mario. He eased his hand away from the knife strap. Jessica swung her arm back, ready to stab the kid with the fatal injection.

The bedside lamps switched on and off, strobing the bedroom, but Mario kept his focus. He tucked away those emotions he so desperately avoided. Fear, rage, despair—they all shook at the bars of his ribcage demanding to be let out.

Not yet.

Each step had to be deliberate and expertly calculated for Mario to get to Jessica before she stabbed the child. Mario leapt onto the bed and launched himself off the other side reaching for Jessica's arm.

The needle was inches from Kira's chest. Jessica's thumb hovered over the syringe plunger, ready to inject as soon as she pierced flesh.

The kid's eyes flinched shut. The bulb in the bedside lamp exploded.

Mario grabbed onto Jessica's arm and crashed into her with all his strength.

The kid's shriek pierced the air, turning to a static background noise as Jessica and Mario wrestled for control of the syringe. The lamp flicked on and off. The walls warped inward.

"It's *him*," Jessica said through clenched teeth as she crawled out of Mario's grip and across the bed. Mario scrambled to grab Jessica by the feet as her front half collapsed over the side of the mattress. She kicked him away.

"Kira, come here!" Sherrie stood in the hall with outstretched arms.

Jessica got to her feet and lunged at Sherrie.

Kira, screaming, covered her ears and shut her eyes. The door to the bedroom slammed shut between Jessica and Sherrie. Mario scrambled across the bed to get to Jessica.

Sherrie banged on the door, but it wouldn't budge.

Jessica turned her back to the closed door and the screaming mother on the other side. Her eyes were back to the kid, hungry for a kill. Mario bear-hugged Jessica, pinning her arms down. With one hand locked around her forearm, he fought for control of the syringe. He thrust his back against the bedroom door and bust it open.

"Go!" he said to the kid. "Get out!"

Kira ran.

All the possibilities of how this would end crashed into each other, like a multi-vehicle wreck in Mario's mind. Sherrie would call the police. He'd kill Jessica. Or maybe Jessica would get loose and kill the child. Maybe if he held Jessica long enough, the police would arrive and they'd all live. They'd find the pigs and the undigested hair and teeth. Then he and Jessica would go to prison. *Death sentence.* The thoughts tangled in a fleeting moment.

He squeezed Jessica's arm so hard, he was certain he'd leave bruises.

She relaxed her grip on the syringe and let it fall to the carpet. "I'm sorry, baby." Her voice shook. She lowered it to a whisper. "We have to get that dead body out of the house. We have to get *them,* too."

Mario kept her back pressed against his body. He needed to get a hand on his blade. His grip on Jessica's arm held steady while he shuffled her toward the bed, away from the syringe on the floor. "I'm going to let you go in a second," he said. "*Think* before you try anything stupid."

He eased up on her arm, and as she stepped away, he went for the knife under his sleeve. Before he could grab it, a sharp sting bit him in the chest. A syringe into his heart. The second syringe that must've been in Jessica's pocket. The bright pink fluid disappeared as she depressed the plunger. Mario let her go and staggered back. The needle scraped cardiac tissue as the syringe swayed back and forth. His knees buckled. He collapsed.

The drug burned his heart. It invaded those dark cavities and disintegrated all the anger and fear he had stowed away for so long, all those emotions he never confronted, never gave a chance to see the light of day. The seizing muscles in his chest shredded his ability to think about anything other than the pain. As his vision tunneled into darkness, he had one fleeting blink of a thought—*hope* that the kid would live.

Kira

The lights all over the house turned on and off. The walls seemed to breathe, caving inward, then bowing out. Drywall cracked and crumbled as the house moaned under the stress.

"What's happening?" Mom pulled Kira by the sleeve as they ran down the stairs.

"I don't know." She was so scared and out of control of her feelings that she couldn't tell if it was her or *Dad*. She had been able to manipulate lights lately, but everything happening now was out of control. All she knew for certain was that something pulled at her, an energy like dad's—the *not-dad* empty sort of thing tugging at her to find it. The lights flickered during dinner when she thought about it. The basement light had turned on when she opened the door and that hook in her gut wanted to pull her down the stairs toward the energy. But she had hesitated.

Kira stopped at the bottom of the steps in the foyer as her mom ran to the front door and opened it. "Kira," she said, reaching out a hand. "Come on!"

"I have to find dad." Kira knew she wouldn't find him alive. She wasn't so naïve to believe he was hiding in the basement, or even locked up. That not-dad energy was something she never felt before. Maybe the not-dad energy got inside of her and closed that door upstairs so Jessica wouldn't hurt Mom. Maybe it was messing with the lights.

"Dad can't help you now," her mom said, rushing to her purse slung over the back of the dining room chair. "We have to get out of this house and call for help." She dug her phone out of the purse and stepped onto the porch.

Jessica appeared at the top of the stairs, hair frazzled, mascara smeared. "Help," she said. "Mario has been abusing me."

"Kira." Mom's voice was laced with desperation. "Come here."

Kira's heart sped up so fast she thought it'd explode. She lifted her eyes to Jessica at the top of the stairs. "Stay away from us!"

Her mom moved backward, but not on her own. Mom's feet dragged along the tiled foyer. A feeble attempt to fight the unseen force by grabbing the doorframe failed. Mom was pulled all the way to the edge of the porch. The front door slammed shut. Jessica flung backward through the air and smacked against a wall.

Dad? That hook in her gut pulled at Kira. The not-dad energy wasn't full of sadness or fear like the night before. It was a calm energy, something wanting to be followed, to be found. She ran toward it, to the basement door. This time, she didn't hesitate to go after it.

"Kira!" Mom banged on the front door.

At least Mom was safer outside. Kira entered the basement and controlled her breathing. Hanging from a chain, a lightbulb lit up. She closed her eyes and focused her energy on the calling. It pulled her to the corner of the basement where a large freezer sat.

Footsteps above. Jessica.

A pounding in Kira's chest implored for her to open the ice chest, to set free the energy inside. For every beat of her heart, there was a hitch that warned the opposite. What would she find? She knew the answer to that, but held onto that sense of hope that she could be wrong.

She honed in on her fear, let it surface, and faced it head-on. The freezer door lifted open, busting the padlock that held it in place. She did it without thinking—or maybe the not-dad energy did it. She'd never been able to move things the way dad could, but maybe it wasn't Dad's energy that had been helping her tonight after all.

Kira's eyes filled with tears as she edged closer to the freezer.

"I wouldn't look in there if I were you," Jessica said from the bottom of the stairs.

Kira whirled to face her. Her body shook so bad her knees vibrated and her teeth chattered.

"Kira!" her mother's muffled voice carried in from outside the house.

"How's he doing all this?" Jessica asked.

"I don't know."

"Tell him to stop!"

"I can't tell him anything." Kira wanted to crumple into a tiny ball and hide away forever.

"You want to be with him? With your dad?" Jessica's lip curled up. Her eyes glassed over like she was going to cry.

Kira's heart skipped at the thought of being with him again.

"You can *all* be together, you know. Like a happy family. You've heard of heaven, right?" Jessica took a step closer.

"No!" Kira shook. The light flickered. "I want you to go away!"

"And I want you to be pig food!" Jessica's eyes shifted around the basement. She kept her hand tucked into her pocket as she took a step closer. She was up to something, Kira knew it. "You like pigs, right?"

"Pig food?" Kira's breath hitched. The tooth she found last night didn't belong to the pig. Her stomach lurched.

"I've been doing this for a long time. Your dad wasn't the first. This can be quick and painless."

Kira stepped closer to the deep freeze and looked in. A man's body, frozen and all color drained from his complexion, curled in the fetal position. Dad's eyes, wide open. His scruff was tipped with frost. Blood stained his chest. Her heart wanted to collapse in on itself. The light clicked off and on. The bulb swung back and forth. Basement shelves rattled. Kira took all her sadness and anger and let it fill her bones until she thought she'd blow up.

"Dad!" The guttural shriek exploded from her core and pierced the basement air like a supernova.

"Your dad was something else, wasn't he?" Jessica said with a quiver in her voice, palms up in surrender, but she held on to a needle between her thumb and pointer finger. "But he can't help you by turning off the lights, can he? There's no way out, sweetie. Just take a breath and it'll be over soon. Don't you want to be with your mom and dad?"

"*Mom's* okay."

"Not for long. Don't think I don't have a plan for *her*. I always have a plan."

A rapid panting shook Kira's body. Tears flowed steadily like a river. She imagined never stopping. She'd end up with canyons scarring her face from how hard she cried. The emotions were so out of control, she wanted to bring the whole house down on her like it was the cardboard dollhouse from school.

The basement walls cracked. Cinderblocks fell out of place. A ceiling joist snapped in half. The house moaned. Kira took all that energy and pulled it inward to the middle of her chest— that space behind her sternum where she felt like puking. She let her rage and despair swim there for a moment.

You are in control of you.

Just like last night, when the twilight sky seemed to collapse in on her, when dad's energy cried out in the darkness and caved in like a singularity, she pulled the walls inward. Except it wasn't her dad making the sky cave in last night, it was *her*.

She was in control.

More wooden beams snapped and dropped to the floor.

Jessica sprinted up the steps. Kira followed.

Jessica threw herself against the back door in the kitchen, but it wouldn't open.

"Kira!" The foyer window up front shattered. Mom.

"Kid, let me go. It was Mario. *Mario* killed your dad. It was all his idea."

"Shut up," Kira said. As much as she wanted to break down and lie on the floor shaking, or to run to her mom for a hug, she didn't. She took those feeling and used them.

"I'm coming, Kira!" Mom said.

She couldn't allow it. Kira forced her mom back. She could feel her energy now. That ferocious protective nature of a bear protecting her cub. Mom was out for blood. She'd never been able to feel anyone but her dad until now. Now, she felt everything. Mom's desperation and fear clawed at her heart. Jessica's energy seeped from her pores. The electric charge in the circuits. The heat of the gas stove. The sirens of the police cars that hadn't come into earshot yet. The energy of the house, the wood, the snorting pigs out back. She connected with it all and had the innate ability to *move* those things through space.

"Your dad was a drunken loser, anyway," Jessica said, sobbing.

With those words, Kira balled up all the energy in the air between them and stretched her arms forward to thrust it at Jessica. Jessica's body flung into the air and crashed against the wall, knocking her out instantly. The blow was so hard, Kira wasn't sure Jessica's heart was beating anymore. The body dropped to the floor. The woman's energy was different now.

Like her dad's when he stopped feeling sad and went blank. It was a not-Jessica energy.

Kira killed her. She fell to her knees and couldn't seem to pull in a breath.

"Kira!" her mom called again, but her muffled voice was too far away.

What did I do?

This house couldn't stay here. She wouldn't be able to live next door. The terrible things that happened to her dad and to the others needed to be obliterated from her memory. But she didn't have the power to do that. She had the power to destroy *things* though. The ache swelled in her heart and she knew exactly what to do.

She pulled her pain inward and then set it loose on the house. It groaned under the stress. The roof buckled in first. Windows shattered. Then the walls. Crepitation of wood and snapping of beams.

"Kira!" Her mom's sadness invaded her heart.

Kira couldn't stay inside and leave her mom behind. She ducked through the crumbling back door as the house fell. Behind her, mindlessly in tow, was Jessica's body, crumpling in on itself. Her face smashed in, bones cracked. Kira didn't mean to, but it just sort of happened.

She screamed and ran away from the house as the outer walls fell in. Jessica's mangled body hovered in the air.

"I hate you!" Kira fell to her knees in the grass. The night seemed to press down on her. The entire mass of the universe crushing in on the house, on Jessica, and on herself. She flung out her arms and sent Jessica's body hurtling away. It smacked against the shed bordering the pig pen and fell into the mud.

Jessica, under the immense pressure of all the surrounding energy, imploded.

The pigs rushed in to investigate.

"Don't touch her! She's bad!" Spit strung between Kira's lips as she screamed. Her eyeballs felt like they could pop out of her head because of the pressure.

"Kira!" Mom ran around the back of the house and grabbed her.

The house laid demolished in a heaping, dusty pile of wood and rubble.

Red and blue police lights flashed on the trees down the road.

"I called for help," Mom said.

"Come on!" Kira ran toward the tree line with her mom behind her.

"Kira, stop!"

She sprinted forward. Mom caught up. "Kira, we aren't the ones that did anything wrong."

Terrified of leaving evidence of what she'd done, Kira zeroed in on the gas stove. *Focus on the energy.* She sparked the gas line. A blast rushed up behind them and they ducked to the ground. Kira's mom crawled on top of her to shield her from debris.

When the bright flare settled down, her mom looked to her. "I didn't know you could…"

"I didn't either."

Her mom grabbed Kira and held her until the police arrived.

The police found Jessica's remains in the pig pen, but there was no explanation for the state of her body. They said Sherrie and Kira Corbin were lucky to get out alive. The remnant teeth and bits of bone of the other victims were found, and the families of those victims finally had that thing called closure that Kira always heard people talking about.

Kira knew things would never be normal for her again. She wondered if the pigs would ever be normal pigs again, or if they'd ever be happy eating hay and apples instead of people. She wondered if she'd ever get the image of Jessica's mushed-in face out of her head. Or if she'd have to live with that as a curse forever.

One thing was for sure: from this point on, there'd be no more flickering lights that Kira didn't intend on flickering. And no more school doll house destructions—at least not by accident.

More than anything, she would miss her dad. But deep down she knew that whenever things went dark, all she had to do was find the light.

A COLD DAY IN HELL

A SILHOUETTE STOOD against a farmhouse window's yellow glow as Jenn turned down the unmarked drive. Whoever it was could have seen Jenn make the turn. The little blue car slid in the snow, but if she slowed down, she'd surely get stuck. She let the car fishtail toward the ditch before regaining control.

A blanket of white covered the pavement and filled the ditch, making it difficult to see the edges of the road. She stayed dead-center between the trees lining the long drive. At the end, the Walter home stood like a black scar in the snow. Secluded by surrounding forest, it was a place she could lay low with the stolen vehicle. The abandoned building, believed by locals to be haunted, would be the last place anyone would look.

The heavy snowfall would cover her tire tracks within the hour, and there'd be no trace that she had ever driven down that road. All she had to do was light a fire and hunker down for the weekend.

The six-bedroom Victorian that once housed Ms. Walter and her eight foster children was creepy and more space than she needed, but it would have to do. The east end, formerly the playroom, had been ravaged by fire years ago. Even though the rest of the place was in good shape, it never underwent repairs, never put on the market, or lived in again.

"What a waste," Jenn said.

A sweet coo came from behind.

"What do you think, baby?" Jenn twisted around. "Wanna live here for a few days?"

She cut the engine. As soon as the wipers stopped, hefty snowflakes coated her windshield, obstructing her view of the house. Inside the car, crystalline formations moved impossibly fast from the edges of the windshield inward. The glass ached under the chill of creeping frost.

The icy air crept through, chilling Jenn to the bone. "Let's get you inside and get a fire going."

Weeks before, she had busted the lock on the front door and left supplies. "I planned good, baby. We got everything we need for the next few days. We're gonna have a good life. I'm gonna be a good mom."

Jenn pulled the car seat from the back and trekked through knee-deep snow to the front porch. Branches creaked under the weight of snow. The groan threatened to break them and send the pieces of wood crashing down. Jenn hurried up the steps, under the cover of the porch awning. Frosted windows shrouded her view into the house.

The bitter cold cut through layers of warm clothing, biting at her skin, scratching to get inside. When she opened the door, an unwelcoming frigid presence in the foyer pushed back. Jenn struggled against the pocket of icy air and forced her way in.

"What the hell was that?"

Jenn had always been a fighter. Whenever life got hard or it didn't pan out to be what she wanted, she made her own opportunities. When her husband left with the kids and the court deemed her an unfit mother, it broke her. But not for long. Her ex said that the day she got one of the kids would be a cold day in Hell. Spending that day in Hell was worth it if she got to prove him wrong. If that meant stealing, so be it.

She lit a fire in the brick fireplace and pulled the baby carrier to the edge of the hearth. "There you go. That better?"

Jenn unzipped her coat, but the wintry air wrapped its tendrils inside, sending a shiver through her body. Her heart and lungs ached from the bitter cold.

"I think it's colder in here than it is out there." She zipped her coat up to the neck.

The baby stared, eyes wide, reflecting the glowing orange fire. Cheeks flush and pink.

Jenn pulled chilled fingers one by one from her gloves. Sharp pain in the tips with each pinch. Hands tremored. The sensation more severe than being submerged in an ice bath.

She reached for the baby and placed the back of her hand on the child's forehead. Heat radiated from the plump little thing.

"You're toasty." Her teeth chattered. Blue fingertips turned numb. Sensation in Jenn's toes vanished. No matter how close she sat to the fire, her skin would not warm.

She tried to cup her hands beneath the baby while it was tucked in the carrier, but the kid squealed at her touch. The child's piercing cries echoed off empty walls.

Jenn unbuckled the harness. As the last buckle unlatched, the front door blasted open from a strong gust. A blustery wind tore through the foyer and into the den. It swirled, taking shape. For a moment, a woman's form appeared in the rolling ice fog. Jenn shook her head, disintegrating the hallucination of the woman, only to see the door waving in the breeze.

Ms. Walter crept into her mind. The woman who lived here before. On the coldest night on record, the Walter house caught fire. Barefoot and barely dressed, Ms. Walter saved every last foster kid from this burning home, even running back inside to grab blankets to keep them warm as they waited for help to arrive. But as Ms. Walter tossed the blankets out of the window, smoke and fire crept up on her, and she perished.

The crazy woman died saving kids that weren't even hers.

Jenn could do that. She could be that mother.

Jenn's feet lost feeling.

"This was a bad idea, baby. We should heat up in the car. Or maybe find another house." Numb lips made it difficult to speak. Tears begged to fill Jenn's eyes, but the sub-zero air wouldn't let them form.

The kid screamed, a pulsing sputtering sob, desperate for help.

"I'm doing better than whoever had you before," Jenn said.

Parents who could leave their children in the backseat of the car, unattended…those were the ones who were *unfit*. Jenn knew she could do better than those people. She could do better this time around than she did with her own kids.

There were countless times she'd see some hurried parent run into a convenience store, leaving their kids in the car. She'd been stalking the gas stations all month, waiting for her opportunity. This evening, as she was about to give up and head to the shelter, her chance presented itself.

A little blue car had pulled up. The man ran into the store, leaving the car running with the baby warm and bundled safely in the back.

"It's okay, baby. We'll go." Words were increasingly difficult to speak as she lost sensation in her face. "Let me check the news first."

Jenn pulled her phone from her pocket. The local news post headlined the stolen blue vehicle and an amber alert. If she drove tonight, she could be spotted. It was too dangerous to leave. But she could at least warm up in the car.

Numb fingers slid under the carrier handle and struggled to form a grip.

The wind gushed through the house, lashing her like a whip. Jenn fought to move the baby, but instead she collapsed to the hearth. She shivered in a fetal ball, muscles and joints locking tight.

Though she was only a foot away from the fire, she couldn't feel the heat.

The blizzard howled. A snaking fog stretched through the room. It wrapped around Jenn, strangling her into paralysis as the image of a woman stood before her. The woman bent over the baby, placing a hand on the carrier. Sirens bled into earshot from somewhere down the road.

The cold sank deeper under Jenn's skin, seizing muscle and bone, squeezing her heart.

Red and blue lights flashed against the frosted windows. Someone knew she was there.

The baby's cries quelled with the ghostly woman's gentle rocking, and the kid's screaming calmed to soft coos.

A fog crystalized over Jenn's eyes, sharp pain stabbed through, solidifying her eyeballs and blurring the vision of first responders as they entered. Jenn took one last breath, which froze in her lungs. Her vision turned to black. All feeling, all ability to love, to steal, to fight…to grab what she wanted out of life, all of it diminished on one cold day in Hell.

VALENTINE'S DAY

TOWERING ORANGE SHELVES blur in my periphery as I pass the new display of lawn mowers and weed whackers. It wasn't long ago that Chris and I hurried out of this aisle together. I am focused on my mission to get in and get out. Straight to self-checkout, I hoist a large wooden-handled axe up to the scanner.

Valentine's Day.

As cliché as it is, it used to be our special day. But there was no "us" anymore. Everything is *his*. Everything that makes me *me*, has been destroyed by him.

Prickling nerves had me on edge all morning. But it's time. Too many years spent in fear. Too many years of mentally crippling abuse. Too many empty apologies and "second chances." I've hurried him out of too many stores, wrangling his violence like a wild beast, protecting innocent bystanders, but never myself. Trapped in a prison by the person who was supposed to be my best friend, my love.

This axe is my way out. He admired its size last month.

In the car, I fill out a card—one with sentiments of love and affection. Sentiments I claimed to be true six years ago. I loved him. God, how I loved him.

A papercut to my tongue as I lick the envelope stings less than his betrayal. It started as tiny hints of jealousy. Then baseless accusations. His temperament snowballed into a nightmare I couldn't seem to escape.

Chris watches from the window as I pull the car into the driveway. Inside, he is probably wondering where I've been. I stayed out longer this morning, practicing. There's gratification these past few months when I came home late and didn't tell him where I'd been. I know him well enough by now that I can avoid physical wrath if I play the timing of my absences just right.

A master of this deceitful game—but it's the only way to have some kind of control over my own life. A life dominated by his emotions.

I step from the vehicle, adjust my shirt over my belt, and exhale.

It's time.

My pulse a rolling boil, bringing waves of nausea through me. I open the hatchback.

The neighbor mows his lawn and gives a wave as he turns the mower around. Across the street, the teenage girl sits with a friend on the porch. All the neighbors who have heard Chris screaming before. They are kind neighbors, who have checked on me when my eyes were red and puffy, arms bruised from a recent scuff with Chris. But I never had the courage to stand up to him. Never had the courage to turn him in. I thought—*I hoped*—he'd change, like he always promised. I loved him once, before he became so controlling. But six years of gradually intensifying abuse chipped away at my sanity.

I push up my coat and shirt sleeves to expose my arm and lean into the back of the vehicle. The cold steel of the axe blade against my forearm raises the hair on the back of my neck. With a swift, calculated slice, I cut through flesh. Fast and deep. A shriek tries to escape, but I bite my tongue and hold it back. Before blood can spill into the back of the vehicle, I press my cotton sleeve into the wound. It absorbs blood and the black fabric turns darker.

The neighbors are blissfully unaware.

Using my sleeve, I do a cursory wipe of the blade and place the axe in a long flower box. I picked it up from the boutique while running errands this morning.

Wet blood warms my arm, but it's concealed under two layers.

"Where have you been?" Chris greets me with contempt at the door.

I present the flower box to him with the card taped to the top. "Happy Valentine's Day."

His face feigns a joyless smile, suppressing the rage I know is scratching to be let out.

Chris sets the box on the table, opens the pink card, and pretends to read it while he asks again, "Where were you all morning?

"Getting your Valentine's gift." I nod to the long white box. Vomit wants to creep up my throat, and for a moment I consider bailing on my plan. "It's our special day. Open it," I say, denying myself the opportunity to give up.

Chris lifts the lid and pulls the six pound axe from the box. "What's this for?" He laughs. His smile is charming, or at least it was, before I learned what monster resides beneath. No. This smile is not a genuine one.

He remembers.

"Is this a joke?" he asks.

"Remember when we were at Home Depot last month?" The vibrato of my nervous voice reveals my anticipation. "You were looking at that axe."

"What the fuck is wrong with you?" Chris, gripping the wooden handle, allows the steel head of the axe to swing to the floor with a thud. He twists the axe, tapping the head against his boot.

My heart beats so hard, I might puke. "What do you mean?"

"Why do you think I would want this?"

Before I can speak, he cuts me off, taking a step closer. "Don't you remember *why* I said I should buy it?" His eyes narrow. Nostrils flared. Coffee and fried egg hangs on his breath as he leans closer to me.

I remember well.

Chris had been certain the gentleman in the mower aisle was checking me out. Before Chris could make a scene, I led him away to the aisle with the axes. He made a joke about this very axe. About how well it would look lodged into that man's head.

My plan is on track. The axe is in his hand. He's furious.

Chris will hurt me. I'm not sure if he'll use the axe, but he's never been shy about throwing punches. He's not a murderer. At least not yet. If I allow things to progress like this for a few more years, it will come to that. But that's *never* going to happen.

I roll up my coat sleeves to expose blood-smeared skin. The wound dribbles fresh blood and it streams down my arm.

"What the hell happened to you?"

"I cut myself." I take a step backward, toward the front door.

"Why?" His pitch rises. Confusion and madness stir behind his eyes.

"You know how I've been coming home late from work a lot lately?"

His shoulder twitches, adjusting the axe in his grip. His lip curls. "Yeah…"

I step back again. "I felt guilty about something, so I cut myself."

The door, ten feet away, may as well be ten miles away. Getting there seems impossible. Maybe I should give up on this attempt to flee.

No. Stop thinking like this.

His jaw clenches. "What are you feeling guilty about?"

Something rational inside of me takes over. Something superior to Chris, and superior to my fear. My pulse calms. My breaths steady, and I wait for Chris's inevitable explosion before I make my move.

Through gritted teeth, he snarls, "What are you feeling guilty about?"

The axe lifts level to his waist. He smacks the side of it against a wall. "I fucking knew it! Who is he?"

Another step back. I adjust my shirt above my belt behind my back.

It's time.

"Who is he?"

Certainly, the neighbors can hear him screaming by now. But perhaps not with the mower going.

"What does it matter?" I ask.

Tears flood his eyes as Chris swings the axe into the drywall.

It's not the first time he's damaged a wall in our home. Patches scar the hallway from where he has thrown fists, and in the kitchen where he has thrown tools. A large patch job in the living room conceals the history of when he threw *me*.

How many concussions can one woman take?

His body is trembling. His fingers adjust their grip on the handle and he taps it against his boot again before raising it to his shoulder.

I back closer to the door.

"Who are you fucking?" he screams, swinging the axe so close, I can smell the metallic blade on the air as it whooshes past my face. The axe smacks into the flat screen. Spider web cracks cover the glass.

I run to the front door and open it, but Chris lingers behind. Chest heaving, he looks up, dragging the axe behind his slow steps.

I need him to come after me. I need him angrier. It won't take much.

"What if I told you it was the guy from the home store?" The lie is sure to bring a bigger reaction. I steady my stance on the porch.

Chris charges toward me

A screech escapes my lips. Before I realize I've started running, I'm at the bottom of the steps. I turn to face him as he lifts his axe in the doorway.

The neighbor has stopped mowing. The girls across the street look up from their phones.

I pull my concealed .22 from behind my back and draw it on Chris.

His rage, his control over me, his hatred will never end. *Never.*

I pull the trigger. Three times. Three hits, center mass. Just like I had been training to shoot twice a week after work for the past few months. I drop the gun, screaming, and collapse to my knees.

My neighbor, whose name I never learned, runs to my side. "Are you okay? Honey, I saw it. I saw him coming after you with that axe!"

Hands shaking, blood dripping from my self-inflicted wound, I fold over in tears. The gash on my arm throbs, sending undulating waves of blood to the cement.

The neighbor is on the phone with dispatch. "She's bleeding. Looks like he got her with the axe before she took the shot. Self-defense. I saw it…"

I stand, knees weak, but heart strong. Chris lies in a pool of blood. It pours from his lifeless body. A body that can no longer inflict fear or pain. Can no longer drain my soul. I will, from now on, be in control of my every day, *my life.*

The crimson puddle absorbs into the warped porch floorboards. Two large tear drop blood stains come together in the shape of a heart.

Valentine's Day.

It's now *my* special day.

PROSPECT NOWHERE

ON THE SAME DESOLATE STRETCH for over an hour, Peyton Livingston's rental car traversed the unmarked, unmapped desert road. He popped the last of the dried cherries into his mouth and let it linger on his tongue for a moment before gnawing off the flesh and spitting the pit out the window. He wished he could roll the damn window up to keep the air conditioning inside, but it wouldn't budge.

His phone rang and Sarah's name glared on the screen.

Shit. "Sarah, I'm glad you called."

"You went without me, didn't you?" Her tone was calm but sharp.

"Went where?"

"You son of a bitch, you did! That's *my* discovery!"

"Calm down."

"If you find *anything*—"

"Relax. There's nothing out here. This was a mistake."

"My analysis was not a mistake. It's in the ground. You saw the readings," she said.

"I saw globs on a map."

"Those globs are there. Honestly, Peyton, what are you going to do if you find it? Do you think you're going to strike it rich? It's not *actually* liquid gold. We can't just scoop up whatever it is and sell it…We were supposed to be a team."

"We *are* a team," said Peyton. "I've got the money, you've got the information."

"And you took that information and ran. I should've known better."

Sarah had been the dramatic type all through college and adult life hadn't changed her much. She was just as naïve as she was back then. After graduation, she had worked for the U.S. Geological Survey and Peyton took over his dad's realty company. He hadn't spoken with her in a few years, so when she called him last week, he wasn't sure what to think. She admitted she should've reported her accidental find to the USGS. Instead, she contacted Peyton about going out west to find out exactly what was on the imagery she collected. She didn't fully explain her theory of what was all over that square mile of desert in New Mexico—oil perhaps, or some raw crude material from the earth that hadn't been discovered yet. Either way, Peyton saw dollar signs and couldn't resist getting a head start.

He changed the subject. "I should've known better than to rent this piece of shit. The window is busted. Can't roll it up!"

"So, are you there yet?"

"I've got to be close. My GPS quit."

"Peyton, turn around, get a hotel, and wait for me to come out next week. You're not cutting me out of this, and you can't research anything you find without me."

"We'll see," he chuckled.

"You spoiled, double-crossing piece of shit," she spit through the phone.

"I'm kidding—"

"All you do is consume. You have to buy everything you can get your hands on, and if you can't buy it, you *take* it. I should've known better than to think you'd be willing to partner on this."

"I promise, *if* I find anything, I'll sit tight right here and wait for you."

She paused and let out an exhausted sigh. "I did some more research on the area. There's no record I can find that the town on the satellite imagery ever existed. There are conspiracy websites about it, like some Bermuda Tri—"

Sarah's voice cut out.

Sunlight beamed through his windshield as the sun lowered in the western sky. Barely able to see the road ahead, he leaned forward, squinting through the blinding light. Though the GPS glitched on his phone, there was only one direction to go on this endless road. *Forward.* The only direction Peyton Livingston ever went.

The cragged branches of an odd cactus appeared ahead. A dusty red streak of dried paint marked the dirt road like a starting line for a race. Beyond it, two wooden beams stood on either side.

Peyton drove between the posts and over the red line in the dirt. Buildings materialized out of the heat wave like an oasis in some old Arabian movie: weathered wooden shacks with cracked boards and busted windows. Tumbleweeds and prickly growths blocked the entrances of what might have been a general store and a local saloon. About a dozen buildings, most in ruins, were marked with red splotches of paint.

According to the maps Sarah had shown him, the globs should be all over this town.

Remnants of covered wagons littered the street along with a dust-covered Model T and a 1940s Thunderbird. Centuries-worth of broken down vehicles had succumbed to the desert's mercy and abandoned their travelers.

He parked his silver Ford Focus in the center of the dirt drive and stepped into the oppressive desert heat. Even if Sarah's readings were wrong, he could turn the ruins of this Wild West town into a tourist attraction of some sort. He pictured a guillotine photo-op at the entrance, rows of eateries, western-themed games, a waterslide to the east, and a hotel with mirrored windows to capture the sprawling desert view. Train rides. Palm trees. It would be an oasis in the middle of nowhere and people would flock to it like it was Vegas.

Out of a gray, weathered shack, a man in dirt-scuffed khakis and a blue polo shirt charged toward him. "Hey!" The man laughed, exposing a set of teeth as orange as his dust-covered skin. "Thank God!"

"Are you all right, man?" Peyton asked to be civil. He was more concerned with the vision of his riches diminishing if this man had already discovered something. Or worse, if he had already bought the land. "I'm Peyton." He extended his hand.

The dusty man staggered closer. "I'm..." He squinted and looked at the ground as if the right words would materialize down there. "Watch your step."

Peyton pulled back, having nearly stepped into a puddle of red sludge. The same muddy, red color marked the buildings and the road at the entrance to town.

"What is that?" Peyton asked.

The man turned his head, attention tuned to something over his shoulder. "Shhh." He covered his ears. "I can't leave."

"Car trouble?"

"No, my car is brand new." The man gestured to a 1990s-era Pontiac Grand Am, cozy beneath a thin layer of dirt.

A crash from inside one of the shacks startled the dust-covered man. He ducked to the side of the Focus for cover, eyeing the silver rental like it was an alien craft. "Nice car."

"What was that?" Peyton asked.

"It's *them*. We should stay out of their way."

"Who?"

The delusional man stared over the hood of the car toward the shack.

"Why are you guys out here?" Peyton asked, trying to get to the bottom of their intentions.

"The red says I have to stay," the dusty man whispered.

"Okay. Look, maybe you should go inside and cool down, or maybe I can give you a ride to a hospital or something."

"It's not the sun. It's the *red*."

"The red....what? You're not making sense." Peyton nodded toward the sludge puddle he nearly stepped in. "Are you talking about this? What is it? Are you here because of it?"

"Don't get it on you, even if it tells you to."

"What are you talking about?" Peyton shook his head, sad for the state of the man's sanity, but relieved that Dusty didn't seem to be a threat to the discovery, whatever it was. "You're lucky I just happened to be coming this way. Your brain is baked. I'll give you a ride out of here."

"I can't leave!" the man snapped. "I leave and I leave and I leave, but when I leave, *they* get worse. And I just keep coming back."

Beyond the busted porch of a tattered shack, a silhouette of a person flashed behind a screen door.

"Who's in there?" Peyton reached for the car door, now concerned for his safety. "Is your friend sick too? Maybe I should go get some help."

"You can't leave! The red says we stay!" Dusty threw himself in front of the driver side door, scrambling to block Peyton from getting in the car. "Please!"

Peyton knocked the man to the side, forcing his way into the car. He locked his doors. But the windows wouldn't roll up. He turned the key and the car rumbled to life.

"Please, don't leave!" Dusty cried, palms planted on the hood.

"I'm going to go get you some help." Peyton wasn't sure if he meant it.

As he pulled forward for a three-point-turn, a scrawny, shirtless man in ragged bell-bottoms exited the shack, scuffing his feet along the creaking wood. The shambles of some old hippie. Eyes so black in the shadows of the porch, they looked empty. Dangling from one of his hands was the leash to a collared orange tabby as gaunt and malnourished as its owner.

Fuck this. Peyton turned the vehicle around. Tires peeled out, kicking up a cloud of dust that obscured the town in his rearview mirror. At the gateway, a small, elderly woman in a red-splattered sack dress held a paintbrush to the wooden beams. A few straggly threads over her shoulders kept her sack dress from dropping to the ground. Her crinkled skin was as weathered and cracked as the ruined town.

Peyton stopped the car between the posts. She dipped her brush into a pool of the red, ink-like substance oozing from the ground. The sludge bubbled and smacked like a tar pit. She sloshed it haphazardly onto the old wood.

Peyton called out the window. "Ma'am, are you okay?"

"I feed it," she said, voice sweet and crackled like his grandmother's.

"Do you know what that stuff is?" he asked as she dipped the paintbrush back into the ground.

"Red says we stay. See?" She smeared more paint onto the beams. "It keeps us here."

The viscous fluid percolated, splattering on the surrounding dirt, not like anything he'd ever seen. A strange undiscovered substance—his liquid gold. He had to get back to where he could get cell service. He needed Sarah, and needed to get these desert squatters out of his town.

"We feed it." The old granny smiled a toothless grin, then stuffed the brush into her mouth.

"Don't eat that!" Peyton shouted, but her vacant gaze stopped him from helping.

Empty eyes accompanied her grinning mouthful of red goo. It dribbled down her chin as Peyton pressed on the gas. He sped away from town with the sun behind him, moving as fast as the little Ford could handle.

Five minutes went by and still no signal. Six minutes and he glanced down to check again. As he looked back up, the sun shone in his eyes. *Impossible.* It was behind him a moment ago.

He pumped the breaks as two wooden beams zoomed by on either side of the road. Two red, wooden beams—the gateway to the town.

Peyton shook his head as if he could jostle himself into understanding, then slowed to a stop. He stepped into the dry, desert heat on the main drive of the same town he had just left.

How the hell did he end up back here without ever making a turn?

Dusty sat by a cactus between two decrepit buildings. Beside him, a gurgling pool of the red substance. Legs crossed, head down, hand holding a paint brush, he made vertical strokes on the trunk.

"What the hell is going on?" Peyton shouted, but Dusty didn't respond. "I thought you said not to get any of that stuff on you." He edged closer, then nudged the man with his foot. "Hey!"

Without looking, Dusty whispered, "I paint it. I feed it." His speech was slurred and expression dazed.

"Why?" Peyton asked.

"It tells me to."

Snapping dried brush crunched behind him. The little goo-eating granny charged through a thicket of thorny overgrowth.

An entanglement of pricker bushes tugged at her thin skin, ripping flesh as she plowed through without flinching.

"My God." Peyton edged away from Dusty and approached the old woman to offer her a hand out of the brush, but she seemed unfazed.

What the hell is wrong with these people? The value of his gold mine decreased in his mind as he considered the toxicity of the red sludge.

Granny exited the throng of pricker bushes and lay down on her back. Dots of blood seeped from scratches on her arms and legs. Swooping her arms over her head and spreading her legs, she made angel shapes in the dust.

Peyton stood in the center of the road while Granny made angels and Dusty painted the cactus.

The shirtless, dirty hippie in the bell-bottoms fell down the steps of the porch nearby. Still clutching the cat's leash in his hand, he squirmed at the base of the steps. As the fallen hippie turned his head, he exposed empty, crusted sockets of dried blood, devoid of eyes. He gagged, but when his lips parted, the red goo spilled from his mouth.

Peyton staggered backward, scuffing his feet, which seemed to alert the eyeless man to his presence. Hurling forward, the hippie spewed scarlet vomit onto the ground, while the tethered orange cat yowled.

Peyton backed into the Focus and slipped inside, hoping to go unnoticed.

This is a fucking Hazmat situation.

He needed Sarah.

As he started the car, a slender woman at least six feet tall, burst through the screen door. It slammed shut behind her.

Wearing a dingy, blue-gray poodle skirt and a frayed sweater that hung like drapery on her scant frame, she lurched down the steps carrying a gleaming cleaver in her bony hands.

Peyton kicked the car in reverse and sped out of town. The emergency dial option on his phone faltered.

A quick glance at the clock. He'd been driving for five minutes. Hands still shaking, he pressed on, this time clear of his direction.

No turns. No curves in the road. A straight line.

Sunlight at his back.

Six minutes. He picked up his phone to check for a signal.

Nothing.

His car blasted between the two red beams once again.

"No!" he shouted, pounding his fists against the steering wheel. He ripped down the main street, looking for an exit out the other side of the town. No way in Hell was he stopping again.

Outside, the people gathered together as if unaware of each other's presence. Granny chewed on a paintbrush, scratching at dried blood on her arms.

Dusty had moved on from painting the cactus, and walked circles around the body of the shirtless hippie as the slender woman swung her cleaver into the belly of the dead man. Red splattered across their faces. The orange tabby howled as Peyton pressed on.

"Red says we stay!" Dusty shouted, but his voice faded in the dust storm behind the car.

Beyond the last shack at the town's limits, an exit. A dirt road to anywhere but here, barred only by the rotting rust-colored board across the path. The car busted through with ease, then cut across the overgrown passage. Cracking brush tangled beneath the car. He didn't know where this path went, but at least it wouldn't—

Without a blink of the eye, without looking at his phone, the wooden beams encroached as he took his foot off the gas and rolled through gateway back into town.

Peyton shifted the car into park. Gripped the wheel at ten and two o'clock. Focused on breathing. Focused on trying to wake up from this nightmare.

The car quaked as Granny charged head-first into the driver's side, ramming it like a bull.

Her red stained hands reached in Peyton's open window. Dried bits of blood stippled her arms. She grabbed for him with eager fingers.

He let out a scream as he scrambled to the passenger seat, pressing his back against the door, out of her reach.

She retreated from the car, only to charge into the door again. The Focus rocked and she fell to the ground.

Peyton took the opportunity to stagger out the other side.

Blood spilled from Granny's forehead. Wiping it with the back of her hand, she smiled. "Red." She smeared her blood across the surface of the silver car.

While Granny painted the car with her blood, Dusty stood barefoot in the scorching sand as if it were as cool as evening summer grass. With a pail of red slop held over his head, he gave it a tilt. The contents dumped onto his head and down his body, drenching him. He rubbed it all over, scrubbing his armpits and chest as if showering.

The man's mental state deteriorated further each time Peyton left and returned. Exactly what the deranged guy had said when Peyton first entered town.

If I leave, they get worse.

Peyton, hands on his head, world spiraling out of control, out of focus, was stuck in this torturous town. The red stuff was poison. Capitalizing on his discovery looked bleak, but he was Peyton Fucking Livingston and he'd have to find a way.

Think, damn it!

Pools of the red substance peppered the ground and whispered to him...*consume.*

The gurgling, scarlet puddle lured him closer. As he crouched over the living, pulsing thing, an urge within admonished him to reach inside—a temptation so strong it was as if the goo had *told* him to touch it.

To spread it. To feed on it.

He careened away, trying to make sense of his thoughts, denying the red sludge its wish.

Peyton took cover on a porch as the strange stuff demanded him to paint.

To stay. To feed.

Hands over his ears couldn't keep the invasive voice out of his head.

He needed Sarah. He needed his teammate. He never should have come without her.

The slender woman with the cleaver lurched out from behind a structure across the way. Behind her, the remains of the gutted, dead hippie lay face down with a chain around his neck. Tendrils of intestine and torn flesh gathered dirt as she dragged him, body jerking forward a couple feet with each tug on the chain. On top of his body, still leashed to the corpse's wrist, the orange tabby sat like an Egyptian king. The cat's head tilted to one side, nearly falling over with each tug of the chain.

Red sludge spilled from under the dead man's belly, leaving a red-brown carpet trail in the dirt. She dragged his body across the road and behind the line of dilapidated buildings.

Back there, dozens of old vehicles were sprawled across the desert. Wagons and chassis of decades-old cars. Among them laid countless scattered bones. Skulls. Hundreds of skeletal remains—animal and human—had been left to rot in this junkyard cemetery. All memory of who or what they were had been devoured and bleached by the desert into ash white bone.

The slender woman dragged the hippie into a trench of the Red and left him. "We feed it," she slurred, then shuffled back toward the shacks.

Tiny crimson pools mottled the ground. They popped and blistered, summoning Peyton to assist. The flesh of the hippie decayed before his eyes as the Red consumed him, like it had consumed the flesh of all the others before.

Peyton left the field of bones and curled himself into the corner of a porch, awaiting a sundown that never came. The townsfolk continued to pace and paint. They swung their fists and cleavers like rabid creatures lost in their own fried brains.

Time stood still that afternoon while he hid from the desert's mind-melting grip. And he hid from the woman with the cleaver. Most importantly, he hid from the whispering Red.

It urged him to stay, to feed, to paint the barriers that would keep travelers in.

Thumping music cut through the dead quiet of the desert and brought with it a dust cloud. A blue van drove toward the town.

Peyton charged off the porch to meet up with the vehicle as it drove through the gateway and rolled to a stop. He put his hands on the hood, ecstatic that someone could finally help him.

A young woman cracked her window. "Peyton!"

The name was familiar.

"I need help. I'm stuck," he said. "I'm—" His name, his memory, all that he thought he knew, had faded away, bleached dry like the graveyard bones. It was there at the tip of his tongue, but he couldn't retrieve it. "I came here earlier and—"

"Peyton," she said, stepping out of the vehicle. "It's me, Sarah."

He squinted, focusing on the dirt below, trying to remember.

"Jesus, you need help. I haven't heard from you in over a week. Have you been here the whole time?"

How long had he been there? There were no sunsets. No nightfall.

Hands against his temples, trying to remember something, anything, he squeezed. The sludge boiled, urging him to stay, and to make the guest stay.

"What is that?" The woman called Sarah pointed to his hands.

Stains on his fingers. "It's the Red."

Dusty, coated in a crust of brown-red goo, walked into the wall of the shed nearby. He backed up and walked into it again. And again.

Sarah edged closer to the van. "Who is that?" she asked. "Come on, Peyton. I'll get you to a hospital. You're suffering heat stroke or something."

"It's not the sun," he whispered.

The Red whispered back. His eyes shifted, wondering if this woman heard it too. "You can't leave." He grabbed her by her wrist.

She struggled away. "What are you talking about?"

Dusty turned to face them. The whites of his eyes were prominent against his red face.

"Peyton, let's go." Sarah dove into her van.

"If you leave, *they* get worse! *I'll* get worse!"

"You'll get worse if you stay out here."

Dusty charged toward her van and Sarah screamed as she peeled away. She stopped between the posts and called back. "Peyton, get in!"

"I can't."

The car kicked up a nebula of dust as it vanished down the road, and from his memory.

He shuffled his feet along the barren drive, and around to the back of the buildings. An orange cat licked at a clump of molten flesh, coated in the Red. Peyton unleashed the creature. Between the skeletal remains of unnamed townsfolk laid an endless supply of rocks. Peyton collected some. He dipped them into a pail of the red sludge. They looked like cherries. He liked cherries.

A blue van sped into town. He'd seen it before, but it didn't matter. A woman rolled down her window and shouted something, but the words were jumbled, fried into an illegible mixture of nonsense.

Peyton held up the rock and called back to her, "We feed it!"

He popped a cherry into his mouth. The pit cracked his teeth as he chewed. He spit it out and popped in another one.

A scream. The revving of her engine. A dust cloud.

A desert-colored cat rubbed against his leg, falling over with each step. Peyton knelt down to stroke him, leaving a splash of Red along his back. The cat stumbled sideways to a porch and rubbed against the wood.

Peyton strolled circles among the bones with a bucket of cherries in hand. Fragmented memories of his former self had long been consumed. They were a team now, symbiotic in nature. He fed on the Red, and the Red fed on him.

ONE YEAR ANNIVERSARY

IF GARY COULD HAVE DEVOURED the remains of his bride without choking on the ashes, he would. The moment he held the urn in his hands, he knew she'd never be close enough to him again. Even when he slept with the cold stainless steel urn against his chest, Kat was never really with him.

On the counter, the top layer of their wedding cake absorbed the radiant heat from the oven and thawed. Tomorrow, on their one-year anniversary, they were supposed to eat the saved portion of their cake, but her unexpected death left Gary to partake in the tradition alone.

The sweet, warm aroma of her memory carried through the house as she expanded with the rising cake in the oven. Gary licked his lips at the thought of her joining him in a manner far more enjoyable than pouring her ashes upon his tongue. When the timer sounded, he extracted the round pan of chocolate cake, risen into a mound at the center. The scent of Kat-infused chocolate was hard to resist. After it cooled, Gary frosted the cake with care, then placed the top tier of their saved wedding cake upon it.

Tomorrow, he would honor the ritual of eating the cake, and Kat would be with him forever.

Before dawn's light reached through the windows, Gary had already dressed. He put on his best suit and Kat's favorite tie and was ready to begin. He held a framed five by seven against his chest. A wedding photo of the cake-cutting ceremony. Instead of feeding each other romantically, they had smooshed cake in each other's faces. He recalled crumbles falling to the floor. Frosting smeared on Kat's chin and cheeks. Her smile through peach and pink frosting made him the happiest man alive back then. He didn't know if he'd ever feel that happy ever again.

Tears trickled down his cheek and his hands trembled as he approached the kitchen, ready for his wife to join him eternally. On the counter, where he had left the two-tiered cake overnight, the pan sat empty. Spongy chocolate remnants covered the counter and floor. Globs and smears of frosting of different colors painted the tiles. He followed a trail of pastel frosting out of the kitchen and into the den. In the pitch black reading room where Kat used to sit with her books late into the night, he flicked the switch. A soft yellow lamp by her favorite reading chair lit the room. Kat sat there, upright and nude.

He couldn't believe it. He wondered for a moment if it was all a terrible nightmare—the accident, the funeral, the last month of grieving. She looked to him and smiled, but there was something strange about her face in this light. A few steps closer seemed to blur the image of her further.

"Kat?" His voice shook. "Tell me it's really you."

Each step revealed what looked like a painting of Kat. As if one of the great renaissance painters had come in the middle of the night to put her there for Gary to admire. But her eyes followed him. Her red lips stretched into a grin. *She was alive.*

Gary grabbed the flannel throw blanket from the edge of the sofa and tossed it over her shoulders and chest. "You must be freezing."

She smelled of sugar-sweet vanilla. Her lips parted, strings of mucus between them—*no, not mucus.* Something else. Gary held a finger to the red stuff stretching between her lips. It was gritty between his fingers and smelled like frosting. He tasted the sugary icing and jumped back.

"Kat, can you talk to me?"

She stared at him, eyes desperate to communicate. He leaned in to listen but no words came from her mouth, only the warm aroma of freshly baked cake escaped.

Heart thumping wildly against his chest, he paced the room, trying to figure out what to do next. She was back, and he had to keep her safe. "I've missed you." Gary wept, doubling over. "I've missed you so much."

Slow as molasses, Kat leaned forward and stood. A thin layer of chocolate cake remained on the chair, glued to it by flesh-colored icing. Gary looked behind her, checking for damage. The entire layer of icing which formed her back was gone. The back of her legs and buttocks, too—stripped of the frosting skin, exposing the porous dark cake beneath, divots and scars from where chunks had fallen off.

Gary's pulse galloped. Mind racing, he held his palms out, unsure how to help her.

The flannel blanket peeled away from her shoulders. Gravity tore it from her breasts, taking a slab of Kat with it. The blanket denuded the buttercream cover from her body and fell to the floor. Nothing remained of her breasts or belly. The nooks and crannies of her cakey insides were exposed.

Gary dove for the blanket, scraping her icing skin into his hands, then smeared it back on her body.

His gut lurched as he painted the crumble-filled frosting haphazardly onto Kat.

Her swirling icing eyes met with his. A gentle side to side of her head told him "no," but he couldn't lose her again. He scooped up all the bits he could and clumsily pressed them to her body. Clumps of cake flesh fell to the floor, so he pressed harder. His hand sank deep into her thigh where warm, moist cake slipped between his fingers. He retracted quickly, but the damage had been done. Kat's leg gave out and she collapsed to the floor. With no bones or muscles to support her, arms couldn't stop her fall. She smashed flat, limbs diminishing to pieces upon impact. She lay with her face to the side, silently pleading.

He knelt beside her wrecked body. The perfect likeness of half a face was the only part left intact. He raised the back of his hand to wipe his tears, smearing cake and frosting across his cheek, nose, and lips.

He licked the sweet bits of dessert away. The delicate taste of his wife on his tongue calmed him. Gary closed his eyes, inserting a finger in his mouth, sucking the sweetness clean. Kat slid down his throat, into his belly. That bit of her would be with him forever.

But it wasn't enough. He needed more of her. He started with the crumbs. On hands and knees he crawled around scooping up her unsalvageable bits. Fistfuls of cake and icing went down his throat. When he finished with the floor, he went to work on the chair, licking it clean. Then he moved on to the blanket. Bits of wooly flannel scraped his teeth as he pulled it from his mouth, sucking it clean. Belly distended, Gary pushed on until every bit of the mess surrounding Kat was inside him.

All that was left of her wasn't much to look at. A single leg and torso. One arm with an outstretched mangled hand. Her head, and the side of her gorgeous face.

Her expression begged him to stop, but he couldn't. The delectable taste of his wife was better than he'd ever imagined. Gary dove in for more. He reached for her hand, which she tried to move away, but her digits barely twitched. Digging his fingers into the spongy cake, Gary ripped her hand away from her arm and shoveled it into his mouth. Frosting smeared across his face and crumbs dropped to the floor around him. Eating his way up her arm, to her shoulder, he came face to face with her. A forlorn expression begged him to stop...or maybe she begged him to get it over with.

Gary ran to the kitchen, slipping in frosting as he scrambled for a knife. He returned by her side and pet her black, glazed hair, leaving finger-grooves in their wake.

He held the butcher's knife to the side of her face. "Happy anniversary, my love." The knife cut straight down in front of her ear, through her spongy head. Kat's face slivered off and landed in his hand. One last kiss to her red lips, and Gary devoured her—every crumb.

No matter how gravid and sick he became, he forced every last bit of his wife into his painful, swollen belly. Gary lay on the floor among the delectable viscera of his wife's remains, content that she would be part of him forever.

TO THE GROUND

LIKE HOUSES, relationships stand on foundations, but the mortar of Tamara and Drake's foundation was made of lies. A week before their wedding, she couldn't let him think she was losing her mind. Unraveling before him would only drive him away.

Tamara drove along an overgrown path between towering pines, pulse propelling her toward an unclear destination. An iron skeleton key dangled on a chain around her neck. From the moment she picked it up, an energy summoned her to the ancestral land.

Last night, a woman came to Tamara in her dreams, pulling her from bed. Drake found her sleepwalking, car keys in hand.

What was she supposed to tell him? That if she didn't follow the calling, she might go insane like her grandmother? Grandma went to the land years ago, found an old foundation and a strange key, but she refused to talk much about it. Before passing away last week, Grandma began raving about the evil land and how the foundation needed to be dug up.

Crazy talk, as mom had said. But Tamara needed to see for herself.

Instead of telling Drake she was mystically drawn to this place, she suggested they get away for a camping trip and explore the abandoned property left in grandma's will.

The 50-acre plot of land was barricaded by thick forest. A castle once stood on this lot, long before her ancestors purchased the land. Along with the strange key, grandma kept documents tucked in an old oak box. They stated the former castle had been torn down, leaving nothing more than a stone foundation. A hundred years later, Carver Arrington built a spacious home over it. Nearly illegible cursive notes on faded frail paper from a doctor read: *Shortly after taking residence, Annabelle Arrington went mad. Delirium took hold. Mrs. Arrington set fire to the home with herself and Mr. Arrington inside.*

The land called her home, and Tamara answered.

"This is it." She stopped the car as it entered a stadium-size field of weeds and wildflowers. If only she could get away from Drake for a while for a cigarette.

They quit smoking together last month. He'd been doing so well, but she caved and started again. Unwilling to come clean out of fear of enticing him, she kept yet another secret from her fiancé. Great way to start a marriage.

"*This* is your family's land?" Drake asked. "This is amazing. Why didn't anyone build something here after the house burned down?"

Tamara's heart answered. A soft whisper escaped her lips. "Unwelcome."

"What?"

She shrugged. "Nothing."

"Whoa, check it out." Drake pointed to the tree line.

Peeking over the tops of grasses and brush, tucked against the wood's shadowy edge, stood the tips of gravestones.

"Carver Arrington." Drake stood before a weathered slab. "And Annabelle Arrington. 1880-1905. Shit, she was barely older than us."

The ancient stone stared back at Tamara, as if it had a secret of its own.

"Do you think it's true, what the paperwork said she did?" Drake asked.

"Burning him alive?" Tamara knew it to be true. She felt it in her core. Deep inside there was a window, a connection whispering from long ago. Tamara nudged Drake's shoulder. "Who does that? Who burns someone alive?"

"Hopefully not you."

"Well then you better get working on your vows." Tamara smirked.

"I'm working on it!"

"What've you got?"

Drake stood tall and cleared his throat. "My dearly beloved..."

"That's not even your line."

A breeze rustled leaves. Branches lashed against each other, creaking as they swayed. The sound turned to a hefty rattle that seemed to fall to earth.

"What's that?" Tamara's pulse quickened.

"It's your great-great-great grandmother telling you *not* to burn me alive."

The rattling wood quieted as Tamara followed the sound. Sideways light from the setting sun highlighted a mound of earth at least shoulder high at the edge of the cemetery. Behind tangled vines, a distinct pattern of wooden planks appeared.

Tamara yanked at the wild brush. A set of double doors hid behind the growth, pressed into the earth. An old padlock connected the rusted handles. She pulled one, the iron fixture broke away from rotted wood. Termites scattered from underneath. Larvae squirmed. Tamara cringed, dropping the hunk of metal.

Drake helped her pry the ancient door open, wood crumbled under their fingers and stagnant air wisped through Tamara's hair. She stepped forward, leaning into the darkness where a set of stone steps lead into the tunnel. Ruins of the old castle.

"It's the gateway to Hell." Drake laughed, backing away. "I'm out." He turned to leave.

The familiar whoosh of an igniting gas stove echoed in the corridor. The sound of flames grew closer, but no fire arose. Deep in the blackness, something came into view. Tamara placed one foot into the tunnel, drawn to the darkness like a magnet. A faint orange glow took shape as a man's face. Her breath caught in her throat. Oval spectacles, thick mustache. Cinched brow, his expression severe. The sound of fire roared into a hissing, *"Leeeeeave."*

Tamara felt the burn of hot air inside her nostrils. She staggered back.

Drake ran to her side.

"Did you—?" She cut herself short before admitting to a hallucination.

Confusion was plastered on Drake's face. "What'd you see? A spider?"

"I heard someone down there," she said.

Drake cocked his head. "Don't mess with me."

"I *saw* someone." She looked into the blackness, trying to make sense of it, but nothing over the past few days made sense. How could she explain she'd seen a face wreathed in fire?

"Hey!" Drake shouted into the void.

"Maybe it was an animal." She didn't know why she said it. There was no mistaking what she had seen.

Drake squinted into the black. "How far do you think it goes?"

Tamara lifted her eyes. A massive blue-grey Victorian house stood in the field before them. The house stood as a looming presence against the fading colors of the field. Two tall turrets and long slender windows. A front porch which spanned the width of the house. The sun had fallen behind the trees, casting the entire acreage in shadow. Their car was parked less than a football field's length away, facing the house.

"Where'd that come from?" Drake stepped away from the tunnel.

The dark windows invited Tamara in. Her heart pounded against the skeleton key.

Drake put his hands on his head. "I thought the house burned down."

"It did…"

"This is creepy."

"It had to have been there," Tamara said, but she didn't believe her words. There was something off about this property.

Drake gestured, mouth agape. "And we didn't see it?"

"Shadows? The sun was setting. An optical illusion? I don't know. Houses don't just appear out of nowhere." With every word spoken, she felt the distance expand between her and Drake.

Drake shook his head. "Nope. We're done here. We'll go to that shitty motel down the road."

Tamara couldn't argue. As much as she felt drawn to the house, another force repelled her. A magnetic north and south pulling and pushing. Drake was right. She needed to get out. Something was very wrong here. But first, a cigarette.

"I need to pee," she lied.

As Drake headed to the car to give her privacy, Tamara stepped into the woods and lit the cigarette she had stashed in her sock. Smoke filled her lungs. She held it for a moment before releasing a cloud above her. Her heart raced as she tried to process what was happening to her and whether she should come clean and tell Drake.

She closed her eyes and envisioned the skeleton key in her hand. *Her heart pounded wildly as she approached what appeared to be shackles in a stone wall.*

"Tamara!" Drake's voice called for her.

She flung the cigarette, which had been smoked down to the filter somehow, and she opened her eyes to darkness. The smell of mildew struck her first. Dank air, musty. She lost all sense of time and space. The glowing end of her cigarette faded on the ground. She was underground. Perhaps in the tunnel. The sound of her breath echoed.

Warmth encompassed her body, as if she were standing in direct sunlight. Thick air filled her lungs making it difficult to inhale. Tamara fumbled her phone out of her pocket for light. She panned the beam, illuminating a fieldstone wall. Soil and roots ate away at old mortar. A dirt floor beneath her. How the hell did she get there?

A black stove sat in the corner, pipes rising from the furnace and disappearing into the floorboards above. Beside it was a pile of firewood, blackening with years of mold and rot.

Tamara shifted her gaze up the wall. The light fell upon two thick chains bolted into the stone. Shackles dangled from the end, locked shut.

"What the hell?"

Her chest ached under the weight of the old key. Her eyes grew heavy, drawing her attention to the floor. Beneath the shackles lay a well-preserved book. As if someone set it there recently. No decay, no layer of dust and filth. She carefully lifted the book.

Her lungs struggled to catch a breath in the suffocating basement. Something scratched at her airway, like the nagging irritation of smoke, but there was nothing burning other than the stub of her cigarette. Sweat dripped from Tamara's hairline and along her cheek. It trickled down her neck and soaked into her t-shirt.

"Tamara!" Drake's muffled voice rang from above.

The unmistakable sound of an igniting fire alerted her to a corner, too black for her light to reach. Deep within the darkness, a glowing presence grew closer.

"Coming!" Tamara backed toward a set of wooden steps leading to an upper level, keeping sight on whatever approached from the corner.

The flickering, morphing glow drew near. A face rushed through the darkness. Eyes engulfed in flame, he charged at Tamara. Outstretched fingers reached for her. The skeleton key defied gravity, lifting from her chest. *"Annabelle, no!"*

Tamara twisted around. Her toes caught on the first step and she crashed forward. Ribs whacked against unforgiving wood. Her back flooded with intense heat as the fiery man approached.

She sprinted up the steps without looking back. At the top, she spilled into a vast foyer—it swallowed her into its cool, shadowy belly. A long winding stairway led to the second floor and a crystal chandelier hung high above. The Arrington house welcomed her.

"What are you doing in here?!" Drake yelled, charging through the front door. He opened his arms and drew her in. "Babe, you okay?"

"I'm fine." Her trembling voice defied her lie.

Drake's nose scrunched up. "Did you come in here to smoke?"

"No!"

"You don't have to lie about it if—" His attention drifted over her shoulder.

Tamara twisted around. Above a fireplace mantle decorated with oil lanterns and dying floral bouquets, a painting hung. A man and woman stood side by side in front of the Arrington house.

"She looks like you. Are those the ancestors?" Drake asked.

Tamara moved closer to the painting. As big as a double-door refrigerator, the oil-on-canvas drew her in. The Arrington house stood against a blue sky. The woman, dressed in a pale yellow dress, stood steely serious with her hands folded in front of her. Annabelle Arrington.

"Burn it to the ground," a faint whisper echoed in her mind. Tamara side-eyed Drake for any sign that he may have heard it, but he didn't react.

The man in the painting wore a thick mustache and oval spectacles. Tamara's heart raced at the sight of him.

"He looks like the guy I saw in the tunnel," Tamara confessed. She had to come clean about something. "And I think I saw him again downstairs."

"I thought you said it was an animal."

"I didn't want to scare you."

"Jesus, this is all so creepy." Drake shuddered and replaced his fear-stricken face with a smile. "Maybe he's a zombie."

"You think I'm nuts."

"I think you got scared and saw something. Happens to me all the time." He edged toward the open stairwell to the basement. "Yo! Is anyone down there?"

What are you doing?"

"Protecting you from…from zombies, I guess."

"Zombies? Is 'protecting your wife from zombies' going to be in your vows?"

"Maybe." Drake faced her, taking both her hands into his. "Babe, I promise to love you and to protect you from zombies."

Tamara's heart sank. Sometimes it felt as though she didn't deserve him.

Floorboards groaned underfoot. Heat radiated through the wood into Tamara's soles.

"Where's that heat coming from?" Drake asked.

"You feel that too?" The weight of the skeleton key tugged at her mind. It needed to be here. Carver Arrington wanted it. He needed it for something.

Drake met her eyes. "We should leave."

They hurried out the front door into darkness.

Drake's voice tremored. "How is it dark already?"

They ran all the way to the car without looking back.

Tamara turned around. "Where'd the house go?" Darkness swallowed the field. No sign of a structure stood against the subtle shapes of trees.

Drake got into the driver seat. "Get in!"

Sweaty palms clung to the found book from the basement. She'd forgotten she was holding it. On the cover, engraved in leather, it read: *Diary of Annabelle Arrington.*

"Tamara!"

She snapped out of her confused state and climbed into the passenger seat.

Headlights shone over tall grasses, but there was no house in sight. Drake frantically spun the car around, but couldn't find the path they drove in on.

"It was here!" Panicked breaths steadied. His fingers clutched the wheel, white-knuckled. He drove to the tree line, but there was no way through. They bumped along the rough terrain, back and forth, searching for a break in the trees, but there was no way out.

"Fucking, ghost house, and now we can't find..." Drake rambled, but Tamara's mind wandered to the calling in her heart.

At least a football field's distance from the house, which appeared yet again, Drake stopped the car. He tapped at the steering wheel, devising a plan to get out. Or perhaps devising a plan to leave his crazy fiancé.

Tamara opened the diary in her lap. There were only a few pages filled out. Mostly illegible scribbles. The rest of the book remained blank. The few lines she could make out read:

On these ancient grounds my dearest husband built...home...evil...

I must not tell Carver about the visions, or my failing memory...

I woke again in the cemetery, uncertain how I arrived.

"That's fucked up," Drake said, leaning over her shoulder. Sweat dripped from his brow.

"I found this in the basement."

"Are you going to tell me why you were down there?" Drake's impatience and fear bled into his tone.

Tamara looked to the page:

This morning, I woke in the cellar...no memory... Nightwalking...visions of fire. ...It must all be burned to the ground. It's the only way.

Tamara closed the diary. "I think I'm losing it."

"Babe, so am I! This place is fucking with our heads."

"I felt it before we came here. I knew there was something wrong." Tears nipped at her eyelids. "But I didn't tell you."

His eyes widened, his voice pitched. "You telling me you knew this place was haunted?"

"No! I just knew I needed to come here. I felt it somehow."

"That doesn't make sense." Drake tugged handfuls of his hair between his fingers.

"I know!"

"None of that matters anyway. All we need to do is get out of here."

Tamara exhaled a steady breath and closed her eyes.

Tears tried to escape.

But she stopped crying long ago. The foundation this home was built upon was evil. Carver knew it when he began building, but the price was too good to turn down. The land was not meant for inhabitants. The evil on these grounds wanted them out, it turned them against each other.

The bad thoughts invaded her dreams, turned them to nightmares of burning flesh and blistering wounds. Turned them to acts of violence against her Carver.

The old castle was incinerated a hundred years before, and this home she had come to love, and then to hate, must burn as well. The grounds wanted it gone.

Tonight, Annabelle woke wandering the basement with only her lantern. How she arrived here was a mystery to her. Annabelle stood before Carver in the basement. His hands chained to the walls—ancient ruins of an old dungeon, where people were tortured. Carver hung limp in the shackles, wrists rubbed raw from hours of struggle, dried blood left tracks down his arms.

"*Annabelle, no." He could hardly lift his head.*

She stared through him, devoid of any feeling. All she felt was a desire to burn it all. It summoned her to do so. They weren't supposed to be there. Annabelle poured oil from her lantern at Carver's feet. He whimpered in his restraints.

She smashed the lantern onto the floor.

"*Anna-babe, please."*

Annabelle produced a long wooden match from her pocket.

"*My dearest, I love you." Carver quivered with sobs.*

"*This place has changed you. As it has me."*

"*I promise, I'll build you a new house. Somewhere else."*

She lit the match.

"*But*—Babe, I promise to love you and to protect you from zombies."

A fog over Tamara's eyes lifted.

The memory once belonging to Annabelle evaporated into reality. Tamara stood in the basement of the old house, a cigarette between her fingers. An oil lantern in her hand.

"Tamara?" Drake cried. He tilted his head to meet her eyes. Shackles around his wrists. "Are you with me?"

"How'd we get down here?" She examined the cigarette between her fingers. "Who did this to you?"

"You got out of the car," he said. "You were in a daze. I followed you up the steps of the house—"

"The house isn't here!" Tamara's heart raced. "How can we be in it? I'm losing my mind."

"It's okay. It's this place." He nodded. "You're about to burn your finger."

Smoked down to the filter, the cherry glowed in the darkness. She flicked the cigarette to the side.

Drake screamed, "No!"

The moment hung in the air for what seemed to be eternity. She hadn't noticed the second oil lantern, smashed to pieces on the stack of firewood. The cigarette flipped through the air and landed on the oil. Tamara's heart plummeted, crashing into her stomach. She should've noticed. She should've seen the wet trail in the dirt leading to Drake's feet, where bits of glass lay shattered.

Flames roared to life.

Tamara lunged for Drake's wrists. The iron shackles locked shut—a rectangular keyhole.

Flames climbed to the ceiling joists and crept overhead. Blistering heat assaulted her face. Fire fought to travel across the dirt floor.

She fumbled the skeleton key from under her blouse. *Maybe*. It slid inside, clinking metal on metal. She turned the key, setting one wrist free.

Annabelle Arrington appeared beside her. In a long nightgown, alive and breathing, skin flushed. Tamara could feel Annabelle's breath on her face as she leaned in and whispered, *"Burn it all down."*

Tears evaporated before having a chance to leave Tamara's ducts. Burning chunks of wood crashed around her. She growled through the pain as she unlocked the second shackle, setting Drake free.

The key dangled from the open shackle as they ran to the steps, hand in hand, but the stairs disappeared in the inferno. Carver Arrington charged down, arms flailing. Encased in a shroud of feathery orange light, he seemed to float, screaming, *"Leeeeave!"*

Flames moved in from all sides. Tamara and Drake staggered, choking on black smoke.

By the woodpile, Annabelle Arrington stood among the blaze, smiling. *"Burn it down. Burn it to the ground."* Her eyes filled with ash. As she opened her mouth, soot and smoke spilled forth.

A draft of cool air brushed Tamara's leg. In the corner of the basement, a dark hole invited her to safety. She yanked at Drake's hand.

They stepped through the broken wall into a cool damp tunnel. Drake used his phone's light to guide them through. Hunched over to avoid hitting their heads on the low stone ceiling, they hurried along the underground corridor as the fire raged behind. The stone walls of the tunnel seemed to close in, the earth pressed through, angry that man had built upon this sacred ground.

A glance over her shoulder revealed the fiery presence of Annabelle Arrington chasing after. Flames ripped away at her clothes, blistering his skin, melting flesh. Hair singed. Lips curled, exposing teeth and bloody bone.

"Go!" Tamara pushed Drake's back.

Drake yanked on her hand as she tripped up the stone steps. He flung a wooden door open. They toppled out of the tunnel into the tall grasses of the cemetery. Before them stood the headstone belonging to Carver and Annabelle Arrington, forever unable to rest in peace.

Gravestones glowed orange in the flames as the Arrington house burned once again.

Drake started the engine and whipped the vehicle around as fast as he could. Trees parted, allowing them to escape. In the mirror, the house faded into blackness, disappearing once again from the living's eyes. At the end of the drive, where the edge of the Arrington Estate met the county road, Drake stopped and took three deep breaths.

Tamara dug through her secret stash under the console and pulled out a pack of cigarettes. Shaking hands fumbled with the pack. Teeth chattering. She side-eyed Drake. "No more secrets...I've been smoking." Tears bit at her lids.

Drake leaned closer and reached for one.

She retracted.

"Don't hold back on me. It's been a hell of a night." He grabbed a cigarette and held it to his nose for a whiff. "We're in this together. No matter what happens."

"Even if I lose my mind and try to burn you alive?" Her quaking voice could barely get the words out.

"Was that you?"

"I don't think so."

Drake's hand shook as he flicked the lighter under her cigarette. "We'll smoke together tonight, and we *will* quit together. We'll stay together through *everything*. When one of us is trapped, the other will be there to set them free. And even when it seems like one of us is going to burn it all to the ground, we'll talk each other through it." Drake chuckled maniacally. "And... I promise to love you and protect you from zombies."

She wrapped her arms around Drake's neck. "Let's get out of here."

The diamond of her engagement ring caught glints of orange and yellow light. Nothing but blackness in the rearview mirror. As they drove away, plumes of smoke billowed from behind the pines in the distance, blocking out starlight. A ghostly conflagration of when Annabelle Arrington had burned it all to the ground.

NEVER HAVE I EVER

AN APP APPEARED on Mercedes' phone that she'd never seen before. It was an image of a finger pressed to red lips.

"What the hell is this?" she asked. "Tara, did you download an app to my phone?"

Her daughter Tara paused on the stairway, glancing over her shoulder from behind long red hair—a buried history emblazoned in those fiery strands. "Really? Why would I download an app to *your* phone?"

Mercedes forged a smile for her two book club friends who stood by the kitchen island, well within earshot.

"All right, sweetheart. Just checking." A brown curl dangled over Mercedes' eyebrow. She tucked it neatly back into place behind a bobby pin, while Tara kept her course upstairs.

Smooth red wine touched Mercedes' lips as she pulled a sip from her crystal stemware. "Does your daughter still give you attitude like this?" she asked Kim.

Kim flipped a page in *Tales of Karma*, this month's book club selection, likely trying to understand what the book was about. Typical of Kim to come unprepared for the discussion. She carefully plumped her thick black curls, held back from her face with a wide blue band. "Hell yes. Why do you think I drink so damn much? Kids." She huffed. "You'd think growing up and going away to college would make them appreciate their parents a little more, but no. Sadie is still a hormonal little bitch."

Mercedes gave a polite chuckle, disgusted with Kim's blatant belligerence toward her own daughter. Social etiquette wasn't something Kim seemed to understand very well.

Kim sipped her Syrah. "At least she got over that Wiccan phase, or whatever that was."

Mercedes nodded with approval, swiping her eyebrow again for a lock of hair she was certain had fallen, but every strand was in place. "Ridiculous...all that witchcraft nonsense. Good thing it was just a phase."

"So much sage." Kim laughed. "The house stunk of it for two years. Spell books and such...So, Tara is done with all that stuff, too?"

"Absolutely." But the truth was Mercedes had no idea what Tara was up to lately. Conversations grew scarce after the accident. After Mike died, Tara graduated high school and spent the summer sulking in her bedroom with her herbs and crystals and whatever she thought would bring back her dad. She barely spoke a word to Mercedes. She needed space. Time to process. Before Mercedes knew it, Tara was gone—moved into the dorms. Tara had been avoiding the house, likely because she couldn't handle her father's absence.

The big, suburban, loving home had transformed into a cold, empty nest in which Mercedes spent far too much time alone with her thoughts. Book club was a nice break from the horrific silence.

Today was the first time she'd seen Tara in months. Most college co-eds were out partying with friends for Spring Break, but Mercedes found hope in the fact that her daughter chose to come home. Back to Mom, where she belonged.

The lights over the kitchen island dimmed, muting the carefully selected colors of the charcuterie board. Mercedes had scoured Pinterest for the most visually stunning, yet simple, arrangements of meats and cheeses. The island became an oasis of Havarti and Camembert, summer sausage, prosciutto, fruits, and wines. Mercedes would force a sense of normalcy back into her home through Martha-Stewart-approved entertaining. After Mike's death, she owed it to herself. And to her daughter.

The bulbs in the shabby-chic overhead lights fought to return to their warm, bright glow.

"Was that a brown out?" Janelle, a forty-year-old blonde bombshell, clutched her gold cross. It dangled in the cleavage of her proudly showcased new breasts, which she kept concealed beneath a conservative blouse when she volunteered full-time with the children's hospital. But every other moment of the day, she had them oiled and displayed like trophies.

White light flashed through the windows, lighting up Janelle's porcelain-pale skin. A second later, a sharp crack of thunder.

Janelle's shriek rolled into laughter. "Sweet Baby Jesus, that scared me."

Another explosive bang pierced the night, shaking the house. Janelle kept her hand tight against her chest.

"I think a transformer blew." Mercedes glared out the window. Streetlamps snuffed out. Torrential rain hammered at the glass while the lights in Mercedes' home dimmed again. "I don't think anyone else is coming out in this weather. It might just be the three of us."

"I didn't know it was going to storm," Janelle said.

A vibration alerted Mercedes back to her phone. The mysterious new app icon blinked. Mercedes clicked, and the screen went black. "Shoot," she said underneath her breath.

"What's wrong?" Kim hovered her plump fingers above the charcuterie board like an alien craft carefully selecting its abductee. Manicured, long purple nails descended for a mini sausage link.

Mercedes set down her wine. "There's a weird app on my phone and when I clicked it—"

"Don't click it!" Kim said. "It could be a virus or something."

"Too late." Mercedes shook her phone, and the blackened screen lit up with red letters reading: *Never Have I Ever...a Game of Truth & Consequence.*

Janelle lingered over Mercedes' shoulder, reading the title aloud. "Ooh, I remember that game."

"Never Have I Ever?" Kim nearly blushed. "That drinking game fucks me up."

Janelle pursed her lips. "Well, if you weren't such a slut back in the day, you wouldn't have to take so many drinks."

Kim's passion pink lips slid into a slippery smile. "Those days are over. I'm a married woman now. A happily married woman."

Happily, my ass. Mercedes had invited Kim's spouse to book club countless times, but Kim never brought her. Kim claimed her wife didn't enjoy reading, but Mercedes—and everyone, for that matter—knew it was because Kim loved being away from her. Every chance Kim would get to take a conference trip out of town, she was there, leaving her wife of eight years at home.

"Oh, you know I'm just kidding about the slut thing," Janelle said. "Golly, I haven't played that game in about twenty years."

"Golly." Kim rolled her eyes.

Janelle continued, "But it's not really a drinking game, you know. Originally, before it was turned into an adult game, you could play on your fingers. You hold up all ten." Janelle's French manicured nails all went up. "If you've committed the never-have-I-ever act, then you drop a finger. First one out of fingers loses—"

"Or wins." Kim looked to Mercedes with a wink. "Our girls used to play like that. With fingers instead of booze."

"Shall we start book club with just the three of us?" Mercedes asked.

"Now I kind of want to play Never Have I Ever," Kim said.

Janelle nodded, blushing. "We really don't know each other all that well, do we? This could be fun."

Mercedes' screen bled from a black background into a deep ocean blue. White lettering appeared. *RULES:*

"Are you serious?" Mercedes let out a sigh and grabbed her glass of wine, caving to her guests' request. "Let's go sit in the den."

Once the charcuterie board and wine had been moved to the coffee table, Mercedes cozied into the worn-leather Lazy-Boy. She hated the thing, but couldn't bring herself to get rid of it, even if it reminded her of her beloved husband. Sometimes when she sat there, it was as if she could still feel his presence. And that was enough for her to be certain that he had forgiven her.

Janelle and Kim sat side by side on the sofa. Seasonal pillows with a daffodil design accented the white Italian leather.

Mercedes read the rules from the screen aloud: "Never Have I Ever is a game of truth and consequences. You'd rather die than reveal your most guarded truths..."

Mercedes tensed, as if the game had outed her. She *would* rather die than tell anyone about the things she had done.

Lights flickered, and the windows went black. A baritone groan—like the sound of a massive sinking ship—seemed to squeeze the walls of the house.

It fell silent.

"Was that thunder?" Janelle asked.

Mercedes maintained her posture and shrugged. She looked back to the screen.

"...so, you must allow the other players to reveal your truths. If you do not, you lose."

"What the hell does that mean?" Kim asked.

"Maybe if you lie, you're out of the game?" Janelle's face twisted in confusion.

"Each player starts with ten counters. On a player's turn, the player states, 'Never have I ever...' and then a statement that is true for the player. If the statement is false for any of the other players, the player for whom the statement is false will lose a counter. The game ends when a player is out of counters OR when all players' most guarded secrets have been revealed."

"How do we know if our most guarded secrets have been revealed?" Janelle asked.

"Who cares?" Kim sat forward on the couch. "It's obvious some preteen made this game and didn't think it through. Let's just play. Fuck the point system, though. This needs to be a drinking game."

Mercedes shook her head. "I haven't played a drinking game since college."

"Me neither!" Kim rubbed her hands together. "Let's do this."

"With a thirty-dollar bottle of Syrah?" Mercedes asked.

A play button appeared on the screen. Mercedes tapped it, and three vertically stacked profile photos replaced it—the social media profile pictures for each of the women. Kim's on top, followed by Mercedes, then Janelle on the bottom.

"What the hell?" Mercedes set the phone on the coffee table and slid it toward her friends. "I think I've been hacked or something. How does it have our pictures?"

Janelle shrugged. "That's how these apps work nowadays. You agree to play, and they get access to your social media stuff. No biggie."

Kim shook her head. "How the hell did it know we are playing?" She pointed a thumb between herself and Janelle.

"Hey, Tara!" Mercedes shouted over her shoulder toward the foyer, hoping her daughter would hear and come downstairs. If anyone would know, it'd be her. That kid loved computers. She did advanced coursework in high school, which allowed her to graduate with certification in cyber security. Even went on to study it in college. "Tara, sweetheart! Can you help us with something?"

"Technology is crazy," Kim said. "Alexa is always listening. These apps get info that way, I bet."

"Maybe." Mercedes was not entirely convinced. It didn't make sense that the app was on her phone at all. How the hell did it get there?

"Look! My picture is glowing." Kim twisted the phone to get a better look. Below her avatar were the words *Never have I ever…*

"Never have I ever…" Kim licked her lips and looked to the ceiling as if the perfect statement would materialize up there. "…finished reading any of the books for book club."

"So, anyone who has finished the books for book club…" Janelle shifted her eyes and held up all her fingers, "…must drop a finger."

"Put your damn hands down, Janelle," Kim said. "This is the drinking game version. If you've finished a book for book club, then take a drink. If you haven't finished a book, then you're safe."

How was Mercedes supposed to host the monthly book club and admit that she hadn't finished reading the selected material? Kim and Janelle may have had the personalities to get away with that kind of behavior, but not Mercedes. She had an image to uphold. She lifted the glass of red to her lips and sipped, looking down her nose at her friends. "Neither of you have ever finished a book for book club?"

On the phone, alongside each picture, were ten counters. Vertical lines—five to the left and five to the right of each woman's avatar. Mercedes clicked on a line, but nothing happened. "How do I make a counter go away?"

Janelle scooted to the edge of the couch to get a better look. "Whatever. We'll just keep track on our fingers."

"We're not playing with our fingers, Janelle. Or the counters." Kim's irritation bled through. "Mercedes, you're up."

"Okay. Let's step it up a notch, eh?" Mercedes eyed her opponents as her avatar's glow pulsed. "Never have I ever…had a one night stand."

"What?" Kim laughed. "You've never had a one-night stand?"

The statement was true. Mercedes met Mike when she was in college. She'd had other partners prior to Mike, but never for only one night. "I was with Mike for twenty years."

"There's no way you—" A chunk of summer sausage dropped from Kim's hand to the floor.

The prospect of the grease staining the carpet had Mercedes on her knees in a fraction of a second.

A shrill screech. Kim cradled her right hand. Blood pooled in her left palm. It overflowed to the floor, seeped into the carpet's white fibers. Between Kim's feet, instead of a fallen sausage, laid a plump, severed finger with purple nails.

Janelle's shrieks joined Kim's. Mercedes leapt to her feet, knocking against the coffee table and spilling her wine.

There goes the carpet. She pushed the shallow thought out of her head while she rushed to the kitchen for a hand towel.

A cacophony of screams echoed off the walls. Mercedes charged into the den and threw a blue and white checkered hand towel onto Kim's hands. Before the towel concealed the gore, Mercedes caught a glimpse of what appeared to be a surgically precise excision through the pointer finger, right above the knuckle.

Kim's eyes were wide and desperate, confused as hell, as Mercedes pressed the towel against her hand.

"What happened?" Mercedes squeezed.

Kim's face drained of color into a pallid, sickly blue. Her scream turned to a stuttering sob as her lungs emptied.

"Stay with me, Kim," Mercedes said.

Janelle backed toward the kitchen, each step in rhythm with her pulsating screams.

"Shut up and dial 911, Janelle!" Mercedes stood over Kim, applying pressure while blood dripped to the floor.

Kim's eyes crossed. Losing consciousness, she collapsed to her side, head thumping against the arm of the couch.

"It doesn't make sense. What happened?"

Janelle dug into her purse for a phone. Tears dragged black mascara down her cheeks. "Maybe there was something sharp in the meat platter. The knife?" Janelle tapped at her phone.

"That little cheese knife?" Mercedes kept a hand on Kim. Warm blood soaked through the towel and contacted Mercedes' skin. She cringed.

On the charcuterie board sat a two-inch dull blade, marred only by remnant smears of soft cheeses. No blood. Even if she had sliced her finger with it, there was no way it could lop off the entire digit.

A million medical conditions flew through Mercedes mind, from gangrene to leprosy to diabetes—people could lose their legs with diabetes, right? It was all outrageous. Nothing about this was medically explicable.

Janelle tapped at her phone with violent urgency. "I can't call out. The emergency thing isn't even working."

"Go get help, then!" Mercedes folded up the corners of the hand towel to add extra layers to the makeshift bandage. With her other hand, she gripped Kim's wrist as tight as she could to reduce blood flow. "Tara!"

No response.

Mercedes' heart thrashed wildly within her ribcage as Janelle ran from one end of the house to the other.

"What the hell are you doing?"

"I can't get out. The door won't open." Janelle dashed through the kitchen toward the back door, heels clicking across tiled floor. "Everything is black out there. It's all black!"

Moron. Mercedes released her hand from tourniquet-duty on Kim's wrist and reached for her phone on the coffee table. With one hand still applying pressure to Kim's towel, she tried to exit the game. The screen wouldn't diminish. A yellow glow around Janelle's avatar undulated to the beat of Kim's weakening pulse.

"Kim?" Mercedes whispered. "Please wake up."

Eyes as blank as a deer in headlights, Janelle ran back into the den.

"Grab another towel. In the kitchen. The stack of cheesecloths," Mercedes said.

Janelle did as instructed and brought a clean cloth.

"Go in the bathroom. Under the sink, there's a first-aid kit. Get it." Mercedes forced herself to remain as collected as possible.

Blood oozed from Kim's nub as Mercedes replaced the blood-soaked hand towel with the fresh white cloth. Gauze and medical tape held it in place. The bleeding gradually slowed.

She released Kim's hand and checked her pulse—slow, but strong. Mercedes dropped to her knees beside the couch. A blood-drained severed finger sat at the edge of a massive crimson stain. The thing was so damn surreal laying on the floor, like an anatomical model of a finger had been stolen right out of a doctor's office and dropped into Mercedes' perfect home. Bone and skin cut with impossibly clean edges, without even a splinter of bone jutting out or a jagged tear of skin. Sliced through with surgical precision.

The carpet was drenched with blood, clots clinging to the fibers. Reminiscent of the day Mercedes so often tried not to think about. She'd been young and dumb. Blood and placenta had seeped into the linoleum cracks of the RV's floor. Tears poured down her face. A newborn baby screamed in the bed, while another baby lay stillborn in her arms. She had been wretched in pain so horrific she wished death would come swoop her away. Mercedes raked the memory out of her mind, swept it beneath the blood-soaked carpet where she didn't have to see it.

While bagging Kim's finger and putting it on ice (that's what you're supposed to do, right?), she tried restarting her phone. The screen defied her.

"Tara!" Mercedes ran to the base of the steps in the foyer. Instead of a pale grey wall with photographs leading up a stairway to the second floor, there was a blackness. An impossible, dark chasm. With trepidation, she edged up the steps, but where the light stopped, she couldn't get through. A black wall of nothingness blocked her path.

"What is happening?" she whispered through dry lips. Mercedes yelled for her daughter, but her voice echoed off the black barrier and pushed Mercedes back down the stairs.

The house was shut tight. Windows blackened. The doors jammed. Beyond the exits was that black nothingness holding her hostage.

"What the fuck is happening?" Mercedes smashed a chair into the foyer window, but it bounced back. Trapped.

"Mercedes! Kim is waking up." Janelle sat with Kim on the couch, fingers rubbing her cross pendant.

Once Kim woke, Mercedes dosed her with some Vicodin to help with the pain. She explained everything. How they couldn't reach the outside world. How they couldn't get upstairs to reach Tara. How they couldn't make a phone call out.

"I don't even know if my daughter is all right up there." Mercedes' eyes filled with tears. "I don't know what to do...I always know what to do."

Her phone buzzed on the table. The screen flashed blue with a countdown clock ticking away in the upper right corner above their avatars.

A pop-up message warned, "The clock is ticking. All truths must be revealed before time is up or game over."

Twenty-eight minutes remained, and one of the vertical lines to the right of Kim's avatar had disappeared.

A wave of nausea slid through Mercedes. All three of the women stared at the phone as she set it on the coffee table. A collective realization.

"That's not possible," Janelle said.

"No shit." Mercedes topped off a glass of Syrah and took a swig. "She lost a counter. Kim's fucking finger." Mercedes steadied her shaking body and handed Kim the glass. "For the pain."

Kim accepted it, trembling.

Mercedes brushed her curl off her face and back beneath the bobby pin.

"So that means Kim had a one-night stand?" Janelle asked.

"Jesus, you're fucking dim," Kim snapped. "That's not exactly something we need to discuss."

Janelle hung her head. "Well, how come nothing happened to Mercedes when you said the thing about finishing the book?"

"Because I lied." Mercedes crossed her arms. "I've always hated this game."

Janelle let out a deep sigh. "Never have I ever—"

"Whoa!" Mercedes held out her hands. "What are you doing?"

"We have to finish or game over," Janelle said.

"What does game over mean?" Kim's face drooped, her eyelids heavy.

"Never have I ever," Janelle continued, "gone to the moon."

Mercedes released a held breath. "Nice, Janelle. But we need a plan. We can't just ask questions until time runs out, can we?"

"Why not?" Janelle asked.

"We need to know where this came from. We need Tara."

"Mom, what's going on down here?" Tara asked from the foyer, looking into the den.

Tara explained that she had passed through from upstairs without noticing the barrier. But she couldn't get back to the second floor, nor could she get out of the house, like the rest of them.

Perhaps whatever was keeping them in was only a one-way barrier. Which meant emergency workers could get inside, potentially, if Mercedes could find a way to contact the outside world. Maybe there was hope.

Mercedes filled Tara in as quickly as possible about the app. About the finger. As insane as it sounded, her daughter listened intently.

The game wouldn't shut off, not even when Tara pulled the battery out of the back of the phone. That little countdown clock kept ticking away. Twenty minutes remained.

"You guys keep playing…just in case." Tara opened a laptop at the kitchen island and went to work on trying to get a connection to the outside world.

"Keep playing? In case of what?" Kim set down her wine glass, her hand shaking violently.

"So, we play with ridiculous 'gone to the moon' statements until Tara can call for help?" Mercedes said.

A terrible plan, but it was the best plan they had.

Kim's avatar glowed. "Okay. Something safe. Something impossible." Kim shrugged. "Never have I ever...murdered someone."

Mercedes' heart plummeted to her gut. Of all the fucking things to say.

She sprinted to the kitchen sink, locking her fingers together. A sharp sting to her left ring finger. A papercut kind of pain that grew deep—deeper than any cut she'd ever had. Blood seeped from the indentation of where her wedding band used to sit.

Last year, she had removed her ring, intentionally dropped it over the wooden beam barrier at the cliff's edge. When she asked for help, Mike had gone over the fence to fetch it.

She grabbed her ring finger and closed her eyes. The digit slid out of place, slippery against a bloody nub. Mercedes' let out a yowl—an animalistic sound that reminded her of her husband's scream when she had pushed him over the edge of the bluff.

Throbbing swells of sharp, grueling pain overpowered her memory and brought her back to the present. She refused to look over her shoulder to see what would surely be the shocked and terrified expressions on her friends' faces. More than anything, she couldn't face Tara.

Mercedes pressed a cheesecloth against her hand and screamed as the excruciating pain intensified. Her vision tunneled. The ring finger fell into the sink with the thud of a fallen chicken wing. She slid to the floor with her back against the counter and focused on her breathing so as not to pass out.

When Mercedes woke, she was on the couch beside Kim, hand bandaged and throbbing.

Tara sat in the La-Z-Boy, her stony face cold and unforgiving. "Do you have something to tell me, Mom?"

Janelle's arms were crossed over her body as she rocked to and fro, clutching her cross and murmuring what sounded like a prayer.

Kim side-eyed Mercedes.

"Don't look at me like that," Mercedes said. "You have no idea what he was going to do."

"What was he going to do, Mom? What was he going to tell me?" Tara asked, without a hint of emotion in her voice.

"What are you talking about, sweetheart?" Mercedes' cold lips went dry.

"Dad said he needed to talk to me about something important, and then he mysteriously fell off a cliff?" She reeled her rising excitement back in. "What was he going to tell me?"

Tears welled in Mercedes' eyes. "Your father was going to do something terrible."

"Lies!" Tara stood up. "Clock's ticking, ladies." She plucked a chunk of Havarti from the meat tray and moved to the kitchen.

"You did this?" Kim gasped. "Of course! You little fucking witchcraft whore!"

Tara turned to face them. Lights behind her hummed to an intense glow and then dimmed. "I'm not the one living with lies."

"You can fix it, can't you?" Janelle asked.

"You have fourteen minutes." Tara popped the cheese into her mouth and spoke with her mouth full. "Trust me, you don't want the game to end without revealing your most guarded secrets." She slid her finger across her throat and shrugged.

"Tara..." Mercedes barely recognized her girl.

"I'm going to fucking kill her!" Kim stood, but she wobbled from the blood loss and sat back on the couch.

"How the hell did you do it?" Mercedes asked. "A cursed game? A cursed app? How is that possible?"

"You wanna spend time talking about it? Okay...well, the barrier was the hardest part, actually. Took years of practice...I had been studying it for a while but never really had a reason to attempt it. It's kind of dangerous." Tara leaned against the counter in the kitchen, glaring into the den toward the phone— the clock counting down to their demise.

Mercedes let out a sigh. She'd drag the game out until the end before revealing anything else. "Never have I ever time-traveled."

Janelle broke into a sob. "I can't take this anymore!"

"You're just wasting time," Tara said. "You have to reveal your truths."

"Never have I ever..." It was Janelle's turn. She sucked in three sharp breaths as tears streamed her face. "I don't want to lose a finger. I quit. I give up." Her tremulous lips could barely get the words out. "I embezzled money from CHKD for my boob job!" Janelle kept her eyes closed and let out a steady breath. "That's it. That's my deepest darkest secr—" Janelle collapsed to the floor.

Mercedes rushed to her side. Janelle lay lifeless, face-down on the floor. No pulse.

Tara gingerly approached. "Is she…" Tara held her hands over her mouth.

Mercedes pulled away. "You killed her."

"No way." Tara dropped to the floor and rolled Janelle to her back. She started CPR. Eyes full of tears, Tara thrust full-force against Janelle's chest. "I didn't mean for this to happen. I didn't really think it would work."

"You knew exactly what you were doing, you selfish little cunt," Kim said.

"Hey!" Mercedes held out a hand to Kim. "She didn't mean to do it. You didn't know, right, Tara?"

Tara pounded on Janelle's heart, but with each passing second, Janelle became more cyanotic. "Please," Tara hissed under her breath. She turned to Mercedes. "Hurry up and finish the game!"

"Turn the game off," Kim said, holding out the phone.

"I can't. It doesn't work that way."

"How does it work, Tara?" Mercedes tried to keep her tone calm.

"I don't really know. It was kind of experimental. Just finish the game! Reveal each other's secrets!"

Mercedes and Kim stared at each other, willing information from the other. There was no way Mercedes would tell her *other* secret. She'd lose every damn one of her fingers before she'd put that kind of pain on Tara. Telling Tara the truth would hurt her more than keeping the secret. And she could never hurt her daughter. It's why Mike had to die.

Tara gave up on Janelle. Genuine tears fell from her eyes. She edged toward the phone on the coffee table. Janelle's avatar was marked with a bold, red "X." Both Mercedes and Kim's were down to nine counters. Eight minutes remained.

"I don't want to lose another finger," Kim said, trembling.

"Then I better reveal your most guarded secret," Mercedes said.

Kim's brow furrowed. "You're still in the game. Why isn't it game over for you? You murdered your husband. Is that not your biggest secret?"

"You shut up about that. I had more than a good enough reason." Mercedes crossed her arms.

"Come on, girl." Kim changed her tone. "Your daughter knows something anyway. No secrets anymore. Give me a clue."

"No fucking way."

"I think we all know, anyway. I mean, look at Tara's hair...Mike wasn't a redhead. Neither are you."

"That doesn't mean anything. Genetics are tricky." A lump in Mercedes' throat swelled. How could this be happening now, after all these years? She and Mike were so careful with the birth certificate.

"Never have I ever..." Kim's voice shook. "...adopted a child."

Mercedes released a breath, pressing her bloodied, bandaged hand into her belly. "Tara is mine. That's ridiculous." Mercedes turned toward Tara. "I gave birth to you in an RV in Oregon. We were traveling the countryside when you came. I have medical records to prove I was pregnant with you. This is absurd. Stop this stupid game!"

Tara wiped her tears away and stood firm. She shook her head. "You told that story so many times, but it's not true, is it?"

"Mercedes," Kim said, "it's your turn. You have to figure out my secret."

"Give me a clue," she said.

"No way. I'm not ending up dead." Kim stared Mercedes down with a ferocious glare then looked to her left hand where she used her thumb to wiggle the band around on her finger. A clue? Of course.

"Never have I ever," Mercedes said, noting only six minutes remained on the clock, "...cheated on my spouse."

A smile jumped onto Kim's face. "Yes!" She let out a sigh of relief that was quickly engulfed by agonizing cries. Holding out her bandaged hand, she gripped her wrist and fell to her knees. "No!"

Somewhere within that bulbous mass of cheesecloth and bandage, another one of Kim's fingers had fallen off.

On the phone, Kim's avatar turned blue. A text box popped up to the left:

"Your biggest secret has been revealed. Congratulations on coming to terms with your truths. Please continue to play until all players' secrets are revealed."

Fresh blood seeped through Kim's bandage. She squeezed her right wrist to cut off circulation. Nostrils flared as Kim fought through the pain to speak. "I have to keep playing?"

Tara edged closer, tears in her eyes. "Time's almost up, Mom. I worry that you'll both die if she doesn't figure it out."

"What the fuck?" Kim's eyes went heavy as she whimpered, her body curled into the fetal position on the couch.

Mercedes tucked her bandaged hand under her arm, chin quivering. "I would rather die…"

"Mom!" Tara shook her head, then sprinted to the foyer closet.

"Mercedes." Kim lowered her tone. "Give it up, babe." Her gaze steady, watery. "It can't be that bad."

Tara returned with a faded manila envelope in her hand and dropped it onto Kim's lap.

"What is that?" Mercedes asked.

"Dad gave it to me before you killed him." Tara's eyes dug daggers into Mercedes' soul. "He wanted to tell me something, but you wouldn't let him."

"He was supposed to burn that!" Mercedes lunged toward Kim, but Tara held her back.

Tara's grip on Mercedes' bandaged hand sent her to her knees in pain.

"You already know?" Mercedes asked. "You already know and still you put me through this? Why?"

Tara released her and held her chin up high. Her breath hitched. "I needed to hear it from you. You needed to realize your truth and stop living this lie."

Kim shuffled through the papers in the file. Inside, Mercedes knew there to be medical files from Mercedes' pregnancy, which would indicate her baby died in the womb a month before she was due. Also, there would be newspaper clippings from nineteen years ago, from a town in New

Hampshire. Kim's hand fell limp on the pile of papers and she glanced at the phone.

Two minutes remained.

"Never have I ever," Kim's upper lip curled, "stolen a baby?" Her eyes met with Mercedes'.

"You have no idea how much I wanted a child…" Mercedes looked away and collapsed to the floor.

She tucked her knees to her chest as she awaited the inevitable. The bite of another severed finger ripped through her nerves. Within her bandage, her pinky finger fell loose, rubbing against blood-wet skin. But the sting of revealing her secret hurt more than any lost limb. She wished she'd drop dead like Janelle instead.

The phone buzzed on the table, but Mercedes didn't care to look.

"It's over," Kim said. She backed out of the den toward the foyer. "I can see outside again. That dark wall thing is gone." Kim grabbed her purse from the coat rack and ran from the house.

Tara, with her head held high, towered above Mercedes. "I'm sorry about Janelle. She didn't deserve to die. And Kim didn't deserve to lose fingers over an affair." Tara shook her head, wiping away tears that wouldn't quit.

Mercedes' heart folded in on itself, more so than the day she learned her baby was dead in the womb. Without her baby, she was nothing. Without a baby—any baby—how could she live? Mike understood her pain all those years ago and let her keep the newborn infant she had snatched from the stroller of an inattentive teen mom in New Hampshire. That girl had no right having a child. Mike understood Mercedes' pain and let her keep Tara. They went on the run across the country in an RV and waited for her body to give birth to the stillborn, so they could replace her with Tara.

Mike went along with it, but guilt ate away at him over time.

Tara dragged a suitcase from the hall and stopped in the foyer. She held up a newspaper clipping and read the headline from nineteen years ago. "'Search is on for a Baby Kidnapped from Stroller in Manchester.' That's me, right?"

Mercedes lay destroyed and helpless on the floor. She couldn't manage to look her daughter in the eye.

"The parents' names are in the article," Tara said. "I'm going out to the East Coast for a while." She tucked the newspaper clipping back into the file under her arm. Tara wiped her face and looked at the family portrait at the base of the stairs. "Was everything a lie?"

"I love you." It was the sincerest truth Mercedes could tell.

Tara brushed her red hair out of her face and looked around her childhood home one last time. She took a step over the threshold and, without looking back, said, "But you love your lies more."

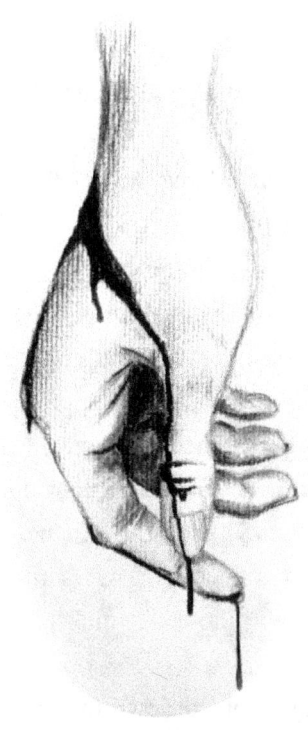

DOLL HOUSE

ALLISON DIDN'T HAVE TO CUT HERSELF open to know she was pretty on the inside. All she ever wanted was for Mama to see it, but Mama had trouble seeing beauty. Cutting remarks about her appearance were far more common than expressions of love.

Looking like TV women is hard work, Mama said. They starved themselves to be skinny, much like Mama starved Allison. Down to half-portion meals twice a day. The *perfect* women had cosmetic work done, just like the dolls lining

Allison's wall, zip-tied in a box with unnaturally tiny waists and perky, pointy breasts, downturned toes delicate like ballerinas.

Instead of affection, Mama gave Allison flawed dolls for her to meticulously carve. Using kitchen knives, razor blades, and melted candle wax, Allison had honed her doll-sculpting skills over the past year, transforming the misshapen things into replicas of the perky ones in the pink boxes from Mama's childhood.

Heavy footsteps marched upstairs. Something dragged across the floorboards. The upstairs door opened, flooding the steps with a wash of daylight. Allison's heart vibrated beneath a dingy purple shirt—unicorn sparkles rubbed off long ago. Harsh fluorescent lights failed to pick up the tiniest glint of remnant glitter.

A woman's body tumbled down the steps, knees over ears, and crashed to the cement floor.

"Got you another doll." Mama's broad shoulders eclipsed the light from the stairway as she came down the steps.

Allison helped her mom lift the woman from the cement onto a pallet in the center of the basement. In Allison's weakened state, her scrawny arms could barely lift a plate of food, let alone a body.

Sunken cheeks and eye sockets made her almost unrecognizable. Bony legs where there once was muscle. Mama said thighs can't touch, so she took away Allison's carbs. Sometimes, Allison would sneak upstairs, unlock the basement door with her pins, and steal a slice of bread.

No matter how hungry Allison got, Mama fed the ends of the bread to the birds. When Allison was little, she used to feed them with her, but Allison didn't get to go outside anymore.

A long time ago, Mama caught Allison feeding a squirrel. She thought they were cute until Mama's toxic glare insisted otherwise.

"They're nothing but ugly rats," Mama had said, laying out poison.

Allison supposed they were a little rat-like. She had watched a medical show once depicting the dissection of a lab rat. Its tiny insides were delicately arranged. Curious if the squirrel was really like a rat on the inside, Allison got ahold of the sharpest kitchen knife she could find and sliced a dead squirrel down the abdomen. The pink, stringy sinew bloomed from the incision, exposing bone and a network of connective tissue. *Beautiful.* Allison had never been so intrigued by beauty. But Mama hated it when Allison exposed the insides. She slapped her across the face after catching her the first time with that squirrel.

Now, Allison would rather have animals again than the dolls Mama brought.

A baseball bat from Mama's high school days knocked the victims out. She didn't call them victims, though. They were *almost dolls*, so close to being pretty. A concussion kept them still and an injection of antifreeze finished them off. Then Mama dragged them to the basement for Allison to *fix*.

A twenty-something woman lay on the red-stained basement pallet, wearing tattered jeans and a tee. Thick, dark hair bundled around the woman's face, round and rosy. Bruises appeared on her cheek bones from the blow to the face. Thin and tall with delicate curves.

Allison couldn't think of a single thing to change.

"What's wrong with her?" Allison asked.

"That freckle is disgusting."

A small brown mole on her cheek created an asymmetry to her face.

"Her hips, too." Mama's upper lip curled.

Allison felt for a pulse, but there was nothing.

"The blow to the head killed her. No antifreeze this time."

Mama pat Allison on the head and hurried back upstairs. The latch clicked.

The door locked for the first time last year. She cried to be let out of the dank dark, but Mama insisted it was the only way to protect her. If the police knew what she had done to Mrs. Brenniman, she'd be taken away. So Allison never screamed for help.

She inspected the woman on the table. Smooth skin. Pretty. Just a raised freckle beneath the right eye.

Mama called moles nasty. Fortunately for Allison, all her face freckles were flat. But sometimes she caught Mama's contempt-ridden eyes staring at her mottled face.

At the end of the pallet, sat a three-story doll house. She unfolded the walls to expose its interior layers. Atrophied arms struggled to pull it apart. Allison would need to steal more bread tonight or she'd waste away. She forced open the dollhouse—no longer for miniature people and furniture. It was a home for her tools. Various knives, razor blades, many too old and jagged to make a smooth incision.

A lit candle melted a pool of tan wax as Allison sifted through her straight-edge razor blades. Sliding tools out of the way, she dug for the best one—the only blade left that wasn't rusted. If all her tools all wore out, maybe Mama would stop bringing her dolls. It had been increasingly difficult to find flaws as Mama's standards approached impossible.

The option of learning something new crept into Allison's daily wishes. She was good at carving and cutting. Maybe she could use her skills for something else. Something *good*. If she learned how to fix bodies the way they're meant to be, rather than how Mama thought they should be, she could become a surgeon someday.

Doctor Allison, plastic surgeon. Or maybe even...*brain surgeon extraordinaire.*

"You look like a...Sara," she said. "Can I call you Sara?"

She pressed the blade to the stranger's face, just below the raised freckle under her eye. The razor's edge depressed healthy skin and sliced through, releasing a trickle of blood. She dragged it in a tight circle, skin tugging at the dull blade. Allison's hand trembled. Frail fingers could hardly hold the tool. Blood pooled at the incision and oozed down the cheek.

Sara moaned under the knife.

Allison jerked back, about to call for Mama, to let her know Sara was still alive, but she held her tongue. Mama often complained of the dolls' lackluster complexions. If she kept her alive, it wouldn't be a problem. This sculpture could be her best yet, and the doll wouldn't have to die.

The spongy mole sat pinched between Allison's feeble fingers, still attached to the woman's face. She focused her energy on steadying the razor blade. It wavered above Sara's face. Allison pulled the mole farther from the skin, attached only by a string of pink flesh.

Just a nick of the razor against that little flesh wire. The metal swiped beneath her pinched fingers and cut the mole loose. Tendon-like string snapped back to Sara's face.

Sara groaned, eyes twitching beneath heavy lids.

Allison dropped the mole to the floor and pulled duct tape from her house of tools. She strapped Sara to the pallet and went back to work.

Detailed smoothing, sculpting like a famous artist, Allison patched the bloody divot with a dab of wax.

Sara's twitching settled and Allison moved on. A perfect, slender neck. Collar bones a lovely shape. Arms lean and strong. Allison sat beside her sculpture, too tired to think about anything but how desperately she needed to eat. But she had to find something to fix or Mama would be mad.

Her eyes drifted down Sara's arms, toward her hands. Veiny.

She'd never fixed blood vessels before. Severing them would only cause pooling of blood under the skin and discoloration. Perhaps if she peeled back the skin, she could figure out what to do with the bulging veins. It was an excellent opportunity to learn a bit of anatomy too. *Doctor Allison— cardiovascular surgeon.*

She lifted the blade, then closed in on the back of Sara's hand. With precision, she cut into flesh. Blood spilled to the floor. From the wrist bone to pinky knuckle, she cut through all layers of skin. Concentrating on the blade's movements, Allison turned the worn tool ninety degrees for a trip across the knuckles. The razor snagged on tough skin. Metal dug down to bone, rising and falling with each mound of the knuckles. She turned another sharp corner back toward the wrist. A rectangular flap on the hand was ready to peel back. It required some strength, but Allison got a grip on the skin flap. A centimeter ripped back with each tug, freeing skin from underlying disuse. She revealed a delicate masterpiece of vessel, tendon, and bone.

Sara twitched as her raw flesh was exposed. Groggy eyes made contact with Allison's. She shifted, trying to sit up, but she was taped securely to the pallet. The moment of realization appeared on Sara's face—that she was restrained. She winced and looked toward her hand where blood pooled in the grooves and between bones before spilling over.

When the women on the table weren't breathing, they were just dolls to Allison. But this one was *alive*, with thoughts and fears.

"Mama?" Allison called.

The woman let loose a shriek that dragged Allison out of doll play and into the gruesome reality before her. Sara's eyes darted around the room. A guttural roar tore up her throat and howled out.

It's not your fault, Allison wanted to say, but all that came out was, "I think you're pretty."

For the first time, Allison felt bad for the doll on her table. It wasn't fair she couldn't meet Mama's standards. With each of Sara's panicked breaths, rationality for all the senseless butchery waned in Allison's mind.

Sara's eyes scanned the room, settling on the bodies against the wall. Her eyes bulged at the sight. Four dolls hung in their upright, casket-sized boxes along the shadowy basement wall.

Women who Mama said weren't pretty enough. Looking at them now, Allison could see how it might be terrifying for poor Sara.

The first was their old neighbor, Mrs. Brenniman. About a year ago, she caught Allison in the back yard with a dead crow on its back, internal organs arranged outside its body into the shape of a rose. A black-winged rose. The sunlight glistened off the moist folds of flesh like dew on petals. Mrs. Brenniman didn't scream. She covered her mouth and tried to back out of the yard, but Allison panicked. She ran to the gate and blocked her from leaving.

"Please don't tell my mama," she begged.

Mama ran out of the kitchen with a steak knife in her hand. A blur of a memory, Mama's hesitation as her eyes darted between the dead crow and Mrs. Brenniman. The knife slitting Mrs. Brenniman's throat. Her head cracking against the pavers. Scarlet poured out of her skull and throat, soaking into the porous stone patio. The memory was splotchy, but not the words Mama said. "Damn it, Allison. Now look what you did!"

"Why'd you kill her, Mama?"

"What if she told someone what you did to that bird?"

"It was already dead. I think it ate your squirrel poison."

"I told you not to be cutting up animals. If anyone finds out how messed up you are, they'll take you away."

"But why'd you kill her?" The question had never been answered.

Instead, they had cleaned the blood from the patio and then dragged Mrs. Brenniman to the basement.

"I'm sorry." Allison's tears soaked into her purple shirt. Fluorescent light lit up the sparkles like fireworks.

"She deserved it." Mama had turned to Mrs. Brenniman's body. "You think you're so perfect." Tears dragged mascara down Mama's cheeks. "Well, your breasts are too big." Mama pulled her steak knife from her apron pocket and cut through her dead neighbor's shirt, exposing her breasts. She stabbed through tissue, slashed out fat from the breasts. Then she moved on to the double chin, which only existed in Mrs. Brenniman's current limp state. She sliced into it, digging out flesh and fat, severing vessels. Blood splattered on the walls, drenched the concrete floor, and soaked through Allison's clothes.

Mama came out of her knife-slashing frenzy and melted to the floor in a pool of Mrs. Brenniman's blood. "It's ugly! It's all so ugly!" She handed the knife over to Allison. "What is wrong with you that you like this sort of stuff?"

"I don't—"

Mama held up a hand, silencing her, then left her alone in the basement to clean up the mess.

Maybe if Mama hadn't recklessly torn through the body, she would've seen that the insides were prettier than that mangled mess. Allison spent the afternoon sewing and wax-sealing Mrs. Brenniman, hoping to earn Mama's forgiveness. Hoping to make her pretty enough for Mama to look at. And when Allison fixed Mrs. Brenniman, Mama approved...and brought her more bodies.

All four of the victims lined the wall. Organs removed to carve the tapered waistlines close to the spine. Breasts had been either downsized by slicing away tissue, or enlarged and lifted with poly-fiber stuffing. Feet narrow and pointy—shaping bone was the hardest for Allison. Without a bone saw, she had to use serrated knifes to cut through. Hack-jobs, but wax helped sculpt a finished look. With Mama's help, all of the women were then zip-tied upright into locker-sized cubbies, painted pink like the pink boxes of Mama's childhood dolls. Tears filled her eyes with each one. "You're getting better," she'd say with a smile. "But not quite perfect."

Sara's screaming brought Mama charging downstairs with a baseball bat over her shoulder. "Why is she *alive*?"

"Mama, don't kill her—"

The bat swiped through the air so fast Allison's hair whipped across her face.

Sara's piercing screams echoed off the basement walls, fluttering around like wild birds. Mama's bat cracked against Sara's temple and the screams crashed into sudden silence.

Panting, Mama nodded toward Sara's hand. The skin was peeled back, blood drooling to the floor. "What the hell are you doing to her hand?"

"They were veiny." Saying it aloud, it sounded insane.

"What does *that* matter?" Mama rubbed the rolling veins of her own hand.

Allison hung her head.

She scanned her daughter and leaned in. "What's that?" Her finger depressed into a soft lump on Allison's chest. Her face went sour, lips downturned. "Are those supposed to be breasts?"

"I don't know." Allison protected her chest with crossed arms.

Mama covered her mouth. "Your butt is getting bigger too." Her eyebrows arched, lips pursed. "And your face. You're getting fatter."

"I'm just growing."

"You're growing the wrong way. Better cut out your dairy now."

"But Mama, I'm hungry!"

Mama's poisonous gaze pierced through her. "Better than being ugly." She pointed to the corpse on the table. "Clean her up." The authoritative command of Mama's voice vibrated through her, screaming through veins, bouncing from bone to bone, insulting every bit as it skittered around.

Mama stormed up the stairs, leaving Allison alone with the dead. Sara lay on the table, skin pale blue, lifeless. Maybe it was all ugly. Allison twisted to get a look at her backside in the blood-splattered mirror. There wasn't much left of it, but she could see the bulge Mama thought was fat. And her breasts were just starting to come in. She imagined slicing open a pocket along the edge of her developing chest, and inserting her butt fat there. Maybe then she'd be perfect enough for her Mama. She could make her freckles go away completely. Burn them off and smooth over the scar tissue with wax.

But on the inside, she knew there was nothing but blood and viscera. Muscle tissue and bone—insides that Mama would never see as anything but ugly.

Allison left Sara's veins alone and closed up her hand. The vessels ceased bulging with the lack of blood flow, but it didn't seem to matter now that her skin wasn't blushing and her heart stopped beating.

"I'm sorry." She glued Sara's mole back in place with a dab of hot wax. "You were perfect as you were."

For the first time in over a year, Allison disobeyed her Mama and went upstairs during the daytime. Scrawny legs carried her up the basement steps. She used her tools to pick the lock one last time. Glaring white light smacked her in the face and she squinted to bring the world into focus. Wood-paneled walls held aluminum framed prints of flowers, but no photos of Allison. The memory of Allison had been wiped clean from the house long ago.

In the living room, pink boxes lined the shelves. Plastic dolls on display. Each one exactly the same. Grotesquely shaped pieces of plastic. Impossible standards for any person to live up to.

Mama slept in the reclining chair. Allison could escape, but she feared Mama would find her, make her keep fixing women who didn't need fixin'. Instead, Allison worked quickly wrapping duct tape around Mama's chest and the back of the chair. She secured her wrists to the armrests.

Mama opened her eyes. "Allison! What are you doing?" She struggled in her binds.

"It smells bad in the basement."

"You can't be up here!"

"But why?"

Mama let out a growl. "Because everyone thinks you went away…Think about what you've done."

"I did what you asked me to do." Her voice trembled. "But it's never enough for you. We need to stop hurting people."

"What do you want? Wanna call the police? Show them what you did to all those ladies?"

"At least I didn't kill nobody!"

Mama shifted her shoulders, but couldn't break free.

"Why did you have to kill them?"

Mama gritted her teeth. "They think they're so perfect. The pretty ones. They think they're sooooo beautiful." She smiled a maniacal grin, saliva stringing from lip to lip. "But they're not!"

Allison stood tall, wiping away tears. "Do you think I'm pretty, Mama?"

"Not when you act like this. Untie me now—"

Allison lifted her knife from the table and pointed it at her mother.

"What are you doing?"

Tears flooded her eyes and ran in a deluge down her cheeks. "Why is nobody ever good enough?" She pressed the tip of the knife against Mama's jugular notch.

Mama stiffened and whispered, "We can fix it. We can fix *you*."

"You can't change what I look like. I won't let you."

"Not what you look like. Your *habits*. Cutting things open. It ain't right. Something's not right with you. We can fix you…on the *inside*." Mama's eyes scanned her.

Maybe there was something wrong with Allison on the inside. Something not right. If she sliced open her own belly, plumes of pink ropes and gushing blood would spill to the floor. It'd be beautiful. But Mama would see otherwise. Mama's eyes ruin everything.

The stainless steel three-inch blade pressed against her mother's cheek. "I think I know what the problem is, Mama."

"We can fix you," Mama repeated, trembling.

Allison set down the knife on the end table and tore a strip of duct tape from the roll. She pressed it to Mama's mouth. "I don't need to be fixed."

Allison grabbed the knife and carefully pressed it into Mama's eye socket, scraping bone at the edge of the brow. Mama's shrill gasp was muffled beneath tape.

She thrashed in the chair, but Allison was careful to work around her jerking movements. She swiped the blade in a circle. It snagged on connective tissue while making a loop—like scooping from a tub of ice cream. With the extraction of the knife, the eyeball plucked from the socket. It dangled there, a faucet of blood gushing around the tethered orb.

Mama passed out from the pain and Allison went to work on the other eye. She cut each one free and dropped the crimson blade into Mama's lap.

"It's not them or me that needed fixin'," she whispered. "It's your *eyes*."

After removing the tape and lying Mama down, Allison bandaged the empty sockets and grabbed the loaf of white bread from the kitchen counter.

She opened the front door. Fresh spring air filled her lungs as she sat on the front step, pulled out a slice, and took a bite. The birds on the telephone wire cawed. Allison tore bits from the ends and tossed them into the yard. "We can both have all the bread we want."

Nothing could hold Allison back now. Nothing could lock her in a basement, starve her, belittle her, and keep her down. She could do anything she wanted—become a doctor or a sculptor.

The world at her feet, possibilities endless, Allison, more than anything, wanted to be loved unconditionally. There had to be a family out there with open arms. A mama with eyes capable of seeing her beauty, every bloody bit of it.

THE TERMINATOR LINE

A HALF MOON HANGS over the patch of forest between me and the man I'm going to kill. A bright semi-circle abruptly ends along a straight line of black. Daddy used to say that's where the Devil lives—along that line in the moon, between light and dark.

He'd say, "Son, most people think the Devil is all the way in the darkness, but he's not. He's right there, on the cusp of wrong-doing."

Shit…who's to say what's *wrong-doing* anymore? Who's to say what I'm doing ain't right? Some people deserve to die. Justice served at the tip of a gleaming blade.

With a hunting knife strapped to my hip, I'm ready to get it over with. It's a hundred-yard hike through the trees and it'll bring me into Greg's backyard. His Halloween party must be in full swing by now.

I slip a latex devil mask over my head. Fitting, I think. Rage surges through my body, devouring any remaining inhibitions. My heart empties of remorse.

A darkness grows in the woods before me, a break in the row of moonlit trees where no light can reach. The abysmal black calls.

Twigs crunch underfoot. My hot, steady breaths fill the latex mask. Blood drains from my neck, shoulders, and legs with each thought of killing that son-of-a-bitch. Branches snag on the black fabric of my Halloween robes, tugging on every step. Each foot forward carries me closer to my purpose. Feeding the rage.

Kill Greg.

As I carefully navigate the ever-darkening woods, my ragged breaths echo in my mask.

The inhale-exhale whispers in cadence, *Kill him. Kill him.*

The voice is confident, determined, but I pause to be sure it's my own. Some other presence is here with me. A glance over my shoulder, through cut-out eye holes, reveals nothing. Scant light from the moon illuminates columns of thin trees, but nothing else.

A light appears in the distant black. A window from Greg's party. My heart shifts into gear, propelling me forward.

The gravelly breaths return, this time they don't come from me, but from somewhere else inside the mask. *Kill him. Kill him.*

I rip the mask from my sweat-soaked head and search for the voice. Only pale trees surround me. They undulate with each breath, branches reaching, grabbing, *pushing* me to carry on. My stomach lurches with the hallucination of the moving landscape. I lean against a pine as roots below swell in sync with my lungs.

"What's wrong with you?" I whisper to myself.

"*Nothing*," the dark voice comes from within. I trace the source down my throat, through blood-drained arteries, to the numb fingers of my right hand. There, clutched in my grasp, is my red, latex devil mask. I hold it in front of me to get a better look. A crimson face, eyeless, glares back. Yellowed horns on top of his skull. Cinched black eyebrows and a pointed goatee ripple in my mind. Two boar-like fangs rise from a jutted jaw, wet with saliva, glistening. The details of the mask come alive in my hands, the flesh making subtle movements.

"*You know what you have to do,*" the mask says.

Tremoring hands nearly drop it, but I hold firm, refusing to believe my eyes and ears. A shake of my head may bring some clarity.

"*Greg has to die.*"

"This is crazy." I wipe sweat from my brow and drop the mask. I'm sick. I have to turn back.

The earth bloats underfoot, sending my body stumbling into a tree. I fall to my side, face to face with the Devil. Its angular features stand bright red against the dark soil.

"I can't kill anyone." My shuddering jaw clenches.

The devil mask sighs. "*Do it for Emily.*"

Emily. My sister is the only reason I'm out here tonight. The memory of her body convulsing in my arms sends a shiver down my spine. She sobbed hysterically after what Greg had done to her. Barely able to speak, Emily confided in me that Greg had blackmailed her into having sex.

"*You remember.*" The Devil grins. "*He deserves it.*"

Maybe—

"*Look at him!*"

The party light grows closer, trees rush by as the Devil brings me to the edge of Greg's property.

From the darkness behind the tree line, I watch as light and music pour from inside Greg's house. Costumed people pass in front of windows, drinks in hand.

"*Look at his smug face.*"

Inside, Greg meanders from woman to woman, eyes penetrating every female in the place. Surely Emily wasn't the first woman he had hurt, and she won't be the last.

The sight of him reignites the fury within. I want nothing more than to cut out his heart.

The hunting knife slips in my sweaty hand, though I don't recall removing it from my belt. Sweat beads on the blade and drips to the ground. I imagine it as Greg's blood, coagulating on the metal and falling to the earth, the ground greedily soaking up his vile existence.

Vengeance pulses through my veins, feeding rage-thirsty vessels.

I'm ready.

Fingers clench the knife's grip so hard they tingle with numbness. The devil mask returns to its place on my head.

Greg wears a white toga sheet as he steps alone onto the back patio—perfect for rolling and disposing of his body. The red glow of Greg's cigarette intensifies in the night.

Kill him.

I approach, breaths stifled by the Devil's intentions, vision restricted by two oval cutouts.

"You scared the shit outta me," Greg chuckles. "Where the hell did you come from?"

"*Kill him,*" the Devil whispers.

Greg takes a step back, eyes glancing toward the knife in my hand.

One plunge of the knife and Emily will be avenged. I raise the blade. One stab into Greg's heart, and Emily will be—

My hand stalls overhead. Emily would never forgive me for such a malicious act.

I lower the blade, wondering if I'd be able to forgive myself. The reflection of the mask in the sliding glass door urges me to continue. I fear if I do, the next time I look in the mirror, I won't see nothing but the Devil looking back.

"*Do it,*" the gravelly voice urges.

I rip the mask from my face. Before letting my rage subside to the point of inaction, and before changing my mind, I throw a hook across Greg's face. His jaw clacks. The impact flings him to the side and he falls to the brick patio.

"That's for my sister." I drop the mask into the grass and fall to my knees while Greg cups a hand around his jaw.

The mask scowls.

Patio light falls upon trees, marking the edge of the dark woods. The place between light and dark summons me to return, begs me to stand at the cusp and consider actions I never considered before.

I lift the blade again, but instead of dealing judgment upon Greg, I plunge the knife into the mask. Tears fall as I retract, then dive in for another stab, and another.

Without me to give the mask shape, the Devil crumples and tears into a voiceless heap of Halloween latex.

In the glow of the half moon, I throw the mangled mask into the woods, and turn my back to the darkness within.

BURDEN'S BEAST

AT THIRTEEN YEARS OLD, Meredith had been taken away. Yanked from childhood, she had been dragged into the depths of some horrifying world that Audra couldn't imagine. Long ago, Audra stopped trying to think of those places her friend could be—those places people don't like to speak of, where young girls are violated and slaughtered. Those places that are so sickening the world turns its head and falls silent in reverence, or fear, or shame. They should be screaming at the top of their lungs. They should be fighting, bloodied and beaten, until those places are no more.

Beyond the empty parking spaces at the Stop-n-Shop, deep in the darkness of the lot, sat a white passenger van. A twisty, repugnant feeling metastasized within Audra every time she saw such a vehicle. Blood curdled and time slowed. Or perhaps time reversed, because an image of her childhood friend Meredith would flash before her. The young girl's black ponytailed hair lashed across her terror-stricken face.

Meredith was nothing but a memory. A faded face on a poster that disintegrated from the telephone poles ages ago. With every passing year, and every passing white van, the cancer of culpability spread through Audra's being for not screaming, for not fighting.

The words *It's all my fault* stained Audra's lips and were tattooed across her barely beating heart.

She stepped into the light of the streetlamp. A plastic bag of purchased items dangled from her fingers. A bottle of red, a magazine, and some snacks. A dry autumn breeze freshened her sweat-soaked athletic wear.

Only three vehicles sat in the parking lot, including the white van parked by Audra's car. Not a person in sight.

She tucked her phone into her leggings' side pocket, readied her keys, and scanned the area. From the safety of the curb, she crouched down for a look beneath the van. Cigarette butts littered the lot. A crushed beer can lay beside a large puddle of oil-laden water with swirls of green, blue, and yellow. No feet lurked on the opposite side of the van. No shadowy figures in hunt of a new victim.

One more skim over the lot and she stepped out of the light. Heart racing, Audra sped across the blacktop. She glimpsed over her shoulder for perpetrators. The weight of the night air swallowed her, drown her in a suffocating panic. She walked a wide arc around the front of the white van to get to her car.

The safe distance wasn't enough to calm her nerves. Body tense, she quickened her pace and clicked the button on her key fob. Yellow lights blinked as her car unlocked. Automatic headlights turned on.

Walking into the confined space between her car and van was not an option, even if it didn't appear that anyone was inside. Her foot splashed into a puddle as Audra crossed in front of her car toward the passenger side, when a deep growl came from behind.

Audra froze mid-step as the snarl skittered up her spine, prickling her fine hairs to attention. The sound transformed into familiar words: *Be quiet and I won't hurt you.*

Body clenched, every cell within in her trapped in a state of arrest, Audra tried to scream, but choked on her own silence.

A large presence encompassed her body, chilling her to the core. As she dug inside to find her voice, her scream was doused by a greasy, wet blanket of fur. It smothered her face.

It yanked her to the cement. Instead of hitting solid ground, she splashed into a basin of murky, black water. The greasy puddle submerged her entire body.

Suspended in the cold, thick fluid, Audra opened her eyes. The blur of a parking lot lamp reflected on the rippling water above. She thrashed until her foot found a spongey bottom. As she kicked off to launch herself to the surface of the impossible pool, the malleable bottom gave under her weight. Her hands reached for the surface, but stopped against an impassable veneer. Frantic fists punched against the plate above. Bubbles from her released breath rolled along the surface as if trapped beneath a sheet of glass.

Red and blue lights flashed above. A man in a uniform, image distorted, crouched beside the pool to investigate. Pounding for attention, Audra screamed for help, her gurgling cries muffled under water. Her call for help was reminiscent of when Meredith had struggled beneath the hand of the gloved stranger.

Despite Audra's attempt to get the policeman's attention, he was unresponsive.

He can't see me.

Audra frantically explored the edges of the spongy cocoon pool, but there was no way out. Chest painful, desperate for a breath, she made another attempt to break through the top. With all of her remaining strength, she kicked off the bottom once more. Instead of propelling upward, her foot plunged through the soft base. Fluid drained around her as she was flushed into the opening below, birthing her into a void of blackness. Gravity pulled Audra and she landed shoulder-first onto unforgiving rock below.

While pulling in gaping breaths, she tucked her injured left arm close, and curled into a ball on her side. Thick, humid fog surrounded her. It filled her mouth and lungs, pungent and acidic on her tongue. She gagged on the toxic air and rolled to her hands and knees to get up.

She was surrounded by utter darkness. Her eyes failed to get some impression of light, or some faint edge of a surface. She reached above for the spongy cocoon, but it was out of reach. She leapt, stretching fingers high, but couldn't find the opening from which she fell.

Icy, cold air escaped her wet lips as she held her lame arm close to her body. Panicked breaths were the only sound she could hear.

She stilled her shivering body and held her lungs closed, quieting her breaths, searching for some audible guide in the darkness. Silence encased her.

Soaked and alone in the cold void, Audra felt her way through the darkness. A wet rocky wall to her left. Another within reach to the right when she leaned. Slime-coated rock—perhaps mold. Audra wiped her fingers on her pants and tried to calm her frantic state. She must have fallen into some sort of cavern system beneath the parking lot.

This doesn't make sense.

Audra dug into her pocket for her phone, hoping the thing would still work despite being submerged in water.

"Wake up," she whispered to herself. Her desperate plea echoed from the depths of the cave.

A girl's voice whispered back, "It's all your fault."

Audra's heart stalled with the faint recollection of the familiar voice.

The phone's glaring screen finally obeyed her fingers and lit up. She directed the light away from herself. She allowed a moment for her eyes to adjust and a faint object took shape nearby in the glow. Audra blinked to refocus. Inches away in the darkness, Meredith's pale face materialized. Her hair was in a ponytail. She looked exactly as she'd looked ten years ago, only more gaunt and sickly. It was the image of how Audra pictured her every day since she disappeared. She'd pictured her curled on one of those dirty, lone beds in a sad room, a single hanging bulb overhead. In her mind, Meredith was tortured and starved.

Audra staggered back, dropping her phone. She dove for it, but when she raised the light, Meredith was gone. Audra twisted herself in circles seeking out the child she saw before.

It can't be her.

She turned on the flashlight function for better lighting, but there was no girl. Blood chugged through her body faster than she could handle, heart working so hard she placed a hand against her chest to keep it from jumping out of her body.

"Audra?" the girl's voice said from the depths of the cave.

A long, rocky corridor stretched in both directions.

Meredith?

"Wake up," Audra uttered through tight lips, trembling. Cradling her phone in her hands, she tried the emergency dial function—nothing. A call to her coworker—nothing.

Down the long cave, where her flashlight beam ended, a form took shape.

Audra steadied her breaths. "Meredith?"

Two conspicuous green lights stared back at her, like the reflective retinae of some animal. A large animal. Audra took a step back, keeping the light aimed toward the creature.

A nose came into sight. She stepped back again.

Greasy, matted fur. Teeth, yellow and fanged.

A wolf perhaps, but far too large. Like a grizzly, but its snout was longer.

Audra edged backward, feeling her way along the wet wall as the beast followed. Its massive body filled the tunnel, proving its dominance.

A bellowing growl rolled through the corridor and crawled into Audra's pores. She ran. Feet splashed in small pools of black sludge. The beast followed behind, shoulders brushing along the ceiling of the cave structure.

Audra closed in on a wall, the end of the tunnel.

Giant, clawed feet took patient, deliberate steps closer. Its gnarled growl echoed through the chamber. The growl slowed and deepened until the sounds split into short pulsing beats. *Click-click-click-click.* Like the clicks of a baseball card in bicycle spokes as it rolls to a stop. Or the branch in the white van's rusted wheel housing as Meredith was stolen away.

The *click-click-click-click* of the beast's slow growl paralyzed Audra into a shivering pile of uselessness.

Do something!

Instead, she froze, backed against the wet rock as the beast neared. Each click of its growl reverberated in the hollow of her gut.

Her phone fell from her grip. With the return of darkness, a fainter light revealed itself in the corner of the dead end. A tunnel, large enough to crawl through.

A way out.

By the time she saw her escape route, the beast was over her. Viscous fluid dripped onto her shoulder. Audra slunk down into a cowering ball as its snout found her in the darkness. Glazed eyes, clouded and dead, reflected the light from the tunnel.

The beast's whiskers scraped along her exposed shins. A tongue, harsh and spiked, licked her leg. A snarling, granular utterance spilled from the creature's mouth, *"Shhhh...Be quiet..."*

Audra shut her eyes tight, whimpering under the beast's hot breath. She obeyed, silencing her heavy breaths, but it didn't matter. Incisors ripped through her skin, tearing away a chunk of flesh from her right shin. Burning, searing pain drew a scream, a screech so loud, it echoed down the cave, bouncing off the walls. The beast roared and swatted, knocking her against the rock.

Audra's body smacked into the wall like a rag doll. Ribs ached. Her arm throbbed. Fiery pain coursed through her torn flesh. Warm and wet with blood, her leg throbbed. Audra, petrified, quelled the need to scream while gauging the distance to her escape hole. She could get inside if she moved quickly enough. Audra lifted her phone from the ground and tucked it back in her pocket.

As the beast pulled back before his next bite, Audra crawled for the opening head first.

Its furious roar vibrated through the rock and into her palms. As she pulled her body inside, it ripped another chunk of meat from her right calf.

Audra's wail, echoic of the beast's howl, muffled as she pulled herself deeper into the cavern. Tears flooded her eyes, but she fought the pain and muscled her body all the way inside. The beast's paws batted through the hole, nicking at the bottoms of her shoes, propelling her forward.

She spilled into a widening and tumbled downhill, head over knees, then sideways. She tried to slow her fall, but the cave's slick rock carried her down with reckless disregard for her pain.

Her momentum came to an abrupt stop as she spilled onto a dirt floor. Audra fought through her pain and scrambled to her feet. Her leg was barely recognizable below the knee—pink, mangled, but no longer bleeding. The flesh throbbed and ached. Balancing on one foot, Audra turned to examine her surroundings.

A square room with walls of cracked drywall. A twin bed in the corner held a bare mattress. Gray, frayed, and stained. Springs rusted and poked through the fabric. The scent of mildew heavy in the warm, wet space. A single hanging bulb in a metal fixture at the center of the room flickered and hummed.

Pain radiated up her thigh as she twisted to see a door. When she turned back, a young girl sat on the bed—*Meredith.*

Meredith's gym shorts and tee—once royal blue and turquoise—had faded into gray, tattered rags. Her black ponytail was dried and matted. Discolored, scarred skin told the story of her abuse—ten years' worth of physical torture was etched into her body. Sadness and defeat lay behind her dull eyes. But she remained unaged. She was still a thirteen year old kid, wearing those shin-length shorts that were way too big for her. She looked exactly as Audra imagined she would.

"Your shorts are so big, you're gonna trip over them," Audra had laughed as they raced to the corner market as kids. Audra blasted ahead, leaving Meredith in the dust. The white van on the curb didn't register until Audra made it to the store. She waited around the corner but Meredith didn't come. When she looked back down the street to see how far behind her friend was, she spotted Meredith talking with a large guy in a hoodie. He towered over her.

Audra headed toward them. The van door was open. Meredith's back was to the door. The stranger stood with his back to Audra. She couldn't see his face straight on, but as she neared, his facial scruff came into view. Dark brown whiskers along the side of his jaw.

The man locked onto Meredith's arm. A scream almost escaped before his gloved hand muffled her call for help.

Audra was close enough to hear him growl, "Be quiet and I won't hurt you."

Meredith's ponytail whipped across her face, throwing a petrified last look toward Audra. An expression that begged her to help. To act. To do something. *Anything.*

But Audra froze. Her body seized with uncontrollable paralysis as the man pulled Meredith into the van and slammed the door.

The van's ignition started and it pulled away, *click-click-click-click*, the branch in the wheel housing sped in sync with her racing heartbeat.

Audra came to her senses and charged into the corner store. Silenced by shock, she choked on her words until finally she released her held breath and screamed for help, but it was too late.

The van was gone. No description of the monster who took her, other than his whiskers. No license plate number. It was all in the past and it didn't take long for everyone to stop talking about it.

"I'm sorry." Audra cried as she sat beside Meredith on the squeaky dilapidated bed. Tears carved canyons into her cheeks, and the pain in her heart became worse than the leg pain.

Meredith sat, pale, malnourished, eyes sunken. Divots in her flesh. Scar tissue covered the wounds. "Why didn't you help me?"

"I don't know. I was just a kid. I was scared." Audra wiped tears away.

"So was I," Meredith said. "This is all your fault."

The words cut deep. Audra had heard them in her head since Meredith vanished. She took a deep breath, remembering what the childhood therapist had told her about the incident—about how it was never her fault. But the therapy never took hold. No matter how much she tried to forgive herself, she couldn't. The blame was forever on Audra.

"Where are we?" Audra asked with a stuttering breath. "What happened to you? How...?" All the questions escaped her with the insolubility of the situation. "Am I dreaming?"

A sweeping sound from the other side of the wall—the beast. Audra backed against the opposite wall near the door. She held her breath as the beast's heavy footsteps passed by, claws ticking on the floor.

Audra checked the door knob, which turned with ease. "It's unlocked!"

Meredith pulled her knees to her chest. "You can't leave this place."

"I'm getting you out of here." Audra opened the door.

The ticking claws of the beast had vanished. She stepped one foot into the damp hallway.

"Be quiet and it won't hurt you," Meredith whispered.

"Look at my leg," Audra said. "It's going to kill us. Look at *you*. Look at your wounds. You can't live like this."

"It'll kill us if we try to leave."

"It'll kill us if we stay."

"*I'm* still here," Meredith said.

"*Are* you though?" Audra pointed her light down the hallway and when she looked back into the room, Meredith was gone.

She squeezed her eyelids shut and focused on breathing. The smell of cool, dry air pulled her out of the room and into the hallway. Throbbing pain realized, it swelled and undulated through her body. Open torn flesh stung in the dank cavern air.

Dirt walls laced with roots and worms lined her path. Soft clay beneath her feet gave cushion to each step. Her wound fired sparks up her leg and into her hip as she traversed the seemingly endless path. Wet shoes squelched and echoed.

In a small puddle of water ahead, a reflection of a face took shape. The forlorn face of a woman rippled in the mud puddle. Audra redirected her light. In the dirt wall of the corridor, a body was buried upright. Face exposed. Eyes closed. Deteriorating.

Another face. And another. Lining both walls of the long corridor were the dead faces of countless victims. Bodies shoulder to shoulder. Some were mere skeletal remains. Others had skin plump and taught. A frizzy-haired woman still had color in her cheeks, as if she were alive.

Audra cupped her hand over her mouth to stifle a gasp.

As she inched closer to the woman buried in the wall, the eyelids opened and the dead thing spoke, "It's all my fault."

Audra stumbled back and swung around as another woman opened her eyes. And another. "It's all my fault," they said.

She tore down the hallway, chased by the deluge of whispers chanting *It's all my fault. It's all my fault. It's all my fault.* As if every woman in history had been buried here, forever clinging to idea that their death, their abuse, their mistreatment was somehow their fault.

Audra ran, faces blurring past as they muttered their chant of self-flagellation. She spilled into an open chasm, a field of alabaster bones. The busted, scattered skeletons and skulls of thousands. In the center, lay the sleeping beast. From his prone position, it was clear that, when standing, it was at least seven feet tall. Greasy, bloodied fur prickled to attention with every breath, then laid flat on exhale.

A pool of light laid beyond the beast, coming from a tunnel. *Daylight.*

Audra stepped into the sea of bones. They clunked together in an alarm like wooden wind chimes, announcing her presence. The beast shivered, but its eyes remained shut as it slumbered.

Audra froze after two steps. If she woke him, she'd die.

Maybe I deserve to die. It's my fault she's here.

She crossed through the bones surrounding the great sleeping creature. Along his flank, there was a wound. Flesh torn away and ribs exposed. Behind those bones, a cavernous void. Something about the void summoned Audra toward it. A force beyond her understanding. A whisper, or some siren inside, luring her closer to the beast.

Encaged within the belly of the great thing, Meredith peered out, hands clenched around the beast's exposed rib bones like she were gripping the bars of a cage.

Bones knocked together as Audra rushed closer.

Meredith grinned and whispered with a gritty voice, "Be quiet." Meredith's face, devoid of emotion, faded away into the blackness of the beast's belly, disintegrating like bits of paper until there was nothing left.

Audra tried to back away, but something held her. A force against her shoulder.

The great beast's teeth sank in, but she hardly felt its bite this time.

For a moment, Audra complied as the great thing ripped the muscle away from her shoulder.

"It's not real," she chanted under her breath. "It's not real." With each chant, the pain lessened, and the attack became surreal, even bearable.

A pink chunk of flesh peeled from her shoulder and disappeared behind the beast's teeth.

How long can I take this?

Ten seconds. Maybe minutes. Or would it be ten years?

The soft voices of the victims in their graves down the hall oozed into earshot. *It's all my fault. It's all my fault.*

Audra snapped from her entranced state. As the beast licked his jowls, Audra curled her lip and snarled, "No! It's *his* fault!"

Body weak, aching and bloodied, she fought through the pain and charged through the bones of thousands toward the tunnel. Bones clacked together as she high-stepped toward a massive burrow which led up to the surface.

Daylight was only a short climb away.

Fingernails collected soil as she grabbed at roots and rock. The beast's growl vibrated in the air around her, but Audra didn't look back. She knew it was there, just behind her, its hot breath at her feet as she fought her way up the tunnel. It was always there, breathing into her pores every day of her life.

The blinding sunlight touched her face.

Almost there.

Mouth wide open, roaring, snarling, *click-click-click-click-click*, the beast closed the gap. Through the beast's voice, the soft sound of the girl whispered through. *It's your fault.* But it wasn't Meredith.

It was never Meredith.

"It's not my fault," Audra screamed, and for the first time in her life, she believed it. She got her footing on a solid protrusion of rock and hoisted herself up. With a grunt and heave, she thrust her torso out of the burrow and into the woods. At the cusp of freedom from the trenches below, from the nightmare behind her, Audra scrabbled out. But as she neared safety, claws sank into her back like meat hooks. Lungs punctured, her ability to scream was stifled. She held tight to the ground as the beast tried to pull her back in.

Nails ripping at her flesh, tearing bloody ravines down her back, she refused to give up.

Audra ripped herself away from the beast. Blood dripped from the creature's nails as it followed her out of the hellish burrow and into the real world.

There'd be no outrunning it. And no hiding. There was no way she could keep quiet and do as it told her. Audra planted her feet and faced the thing, tremoring. It grew, unfolding itself upright onto its hind legs. Front limbs outstretched, intimidating Audra into submission.

Terror wrapped around her chest and squeezed tighter, constricting her breath. Tears streamed down her face. Her heart raced faster with each forced exhale. On the verge of hyperventilation, she huffed through her nostrils like a bull before a fight, trying to regain control over her fear.

But before it could make a move, Audra roared first. From lungs drowning in blood, a horrific, guttural scream spewed forth. An unrecognizable shriek of outrage and courage. She stood her ground and defied everything that he wanted from her. Her imprisonment. Her fear. Her silence. Her guilt. He would have none of it.

The beast thrashed from side to side, swirling into a new form. A smoky, ashen blanket rippled into a whirlwind. It whipped through the air and was sucked toward the earth, retracting into the burrow.

The hole sealed, leaving nothing but a charred patch of earth, and leaving Audra alone in the vast woods.

Her vision blurred as she stumbled to the side, then dropped to her knees. Daylight tunneled into darkness as a man in camouflage ran toward her.

"Ma'am," the hunter yelled, a shotgun held to his side.

Audra fell over, fighting to remain conscious as his sideways blur approached.

"What in the hell was that thing?" he said.

Audra woke under the glare of hospital lights, bruised and beaten. She had black and purple marks where the beast had attacked her, but no blood. No chunks of flesh missing from her leg or shoulder. No claw marks on her back. No measurable internal wounds. Nobody believed her about the beast, despite the marks all over her body. She was questioned about drugs and being under the influence since they found a bottle of wine in her dropped bag from the Stop-n-Shop. Even the hunter, who had seen the beast before it disappeared into the earth, denied it. Fear of judgment crippled his ability to be honest.

But Audra couldn't let it go. She refused this time to let the guilt eat away at her. To let the trail of injustice go stagnant and silent. The beast couldn't be allowed to slink away, all those women buried forever without justice.

Audra screamed, bloodied and beaten, until they listened and dug up the earth in the woods. Meredith's remains were found, but there was no trace of an underground room with a twin bed. No trace of any other bodies. And no sign that there was ever a great beast entrapping them. He'd forever be there, though, in the back of her mind—burrowing deep into all women's minds—growling at them to *be quiet*.

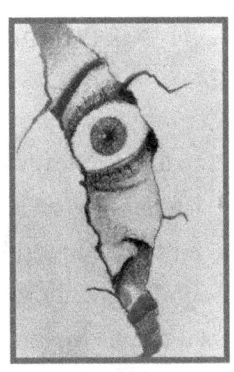

ACKNOWLEDGEMENTS

THE YEAR 2020 STIFLED my creativity when it came to putting out that novel I was working on, but I managed to get my act together and produce a lot of short fiction instead. Simply throwing a pile of stories between a couple covers doesn't make for a great collection, and it's almost never a one-person job. *Dismal Dreams* was made possible by the kindness and support of so many.

Several stories in *Dismal Dreams* were previously published. That means some fabulous editor read my story and thought it was worthy of publication. To those editors and publishers: Perpetual Motion Machine Publishing, Sinister Smile Press, Sliced Up Press, Nico Bell, Laurel Hightower, Gemma Amor, and Cynthia Pelayo...Thank you for taking a chance on me!

I added several other new stories, so an editor was necessary. Not only to edit the *new* stories, but to help polish the others and make for consistent editing style throughout the collection. The fantastic Gabino Iglesias accepted my manuscript and I could not have picked a better person for the job. Gabino made suggestions to improve and polish without taking away from my vision and my voice. He also wrote a jaw-dropping blurb for me that I'll never forget.

For *Lucid Screams*, I wrote my own introduction, but this time around I wanted to do something truly special. I wanted to ask an author whom I admire greatly to write a foreword for *Dismal Dreams*. A special thanks to Sara Tantlinger for saying "yes." I reached out with what had to be the most awkward request for a foreword and she gladly accepted. I'm a big fan of her work—seriously, if you haven't read her stuff, go do that now.

But books without promotion tend to be unread books. Cursed Morsels Podcast, Ink Heist, and TheNecronomi.com invited me to come blab about my book before it released. Thank you!

Then there's the incredibly kind people who accepted my request to read *Dismal Dreams* and write a blurb—Laurel Hightower, Hailey Piper, and Josh Malerman. I asked each of you because you inspire me. At the time of my writing this, you haven't yet written your blurbs, but I'm imagining what they may be and they're glorious. Thank you for taking time with my book!

Before my stories ever make it to publication, they often go through my lovely critique group, beta readers, and proofreaders. The Tidewater Writers critique group is thorough, often doing the work of developmental and line-editors. They nitpick, and tear it apart. They burn it to the ground and help me revive it from the ashes. Lately, since we've only been able to meet online, our numbers have been fewer. Cheers to Tony, Kate, Rick, Melina, and Marilyn. To my mom, Donna, who reads each and every one of my stories, sometimes three times for proofreading. You are the one who inspired me to write in the first place. Thank you.

And to my husband Jason who, when I couldn't seem to finish that novel, suggested that I probably had enough stories for another collection. He was right! Jason, Niam, and Jack— my nuclear family, my pandemic homies—Thank you for being ever-supportive of my crazy dreams.

ABOUT THE AUTHOR

RED LAGOE writes horror, raises kids, and enjoys hanging under the star-studded sky with her telescope. She grew up on 1980's horror movies and even dabbled with some writing as a child, but it wasn't until 2015 that she dove into horror as her genre of choice. She's been bleeding from the fingertips ever since.

Red wrote for Crystal Lake Publishing's *Still Water Bay* dark fiction series, as well as several short stories for publications by Perpetual Motion Machine Publishing, Sinister Smile Press, Burial Day Books, Sliced Up Press, and more. Her horror collection *Lucid Screams* released in 2020 and her debut, zom-poc romance, *Fair Haven* released in 2017.

ww.RedLagoe.com

MORE BY RED:

Lucid Screams: short story collection, independently published with La Red Books, 2020

Fair Haven: a novel, independently published with La Red Books, 2017

Blood Bogged: published by Sci-Fi & Scary, *Twisted Anatomy*, 2021

Black Feathered Fury: published by Sinister Smile Press, *If I Die Before I Wake: Tales of Deadly Women & Retribution,* 2020

Caecillica: published by Sinister Smile Press, *If I Die Before I Wake: Tales of Nightmare Creatures,* 2021

Infectious Glow: published by Sinister Smile Press, *If I Die Before I Wake: Tales of the Otherworldly and Undead,* 2021

www.RedLagoe.com

CONTENT WARNING

Out of respect for those who have experienced severe trauma, the following is a list of topics and their respective stories that may be triggering.

SUICIDE:
(Spoiler)

Dismal Dreams contains a brief, graphic depiction of suicide.

DOMESTIC ABUSE

Valentine's Day depicts a violent, toxic relationship.

MISCARRIAGE
(Spoiler)

Never Have I Ever contains a very brief, but graphic depiction of miscarriage.

CHILD ABUSE

Doll House contains topics of **body dysmorphia**, and child starvation and neglect.